MURDER IN PREEMPTION

ANNE CLEELAND

THE DOYLE & ACTON MYSTERY SERIES IN ORDER:

Murder in Thrall
Murder in Retribution
Murder in Hindsight
Murder in Containment
Murder in All Honour
Murder in Shadow
Murder in Misdirection
Murder in Spite
Murder in Just Cause
Murder in the Blood
Murder in Deep Regret
Murder in Revelation
Murder in Unsound Mind
Murder in Material Gain
Murder in Immunity
Murder in All Fury
Murder in Admonishment
Murder in Protocol
Murder in Reproach
Murder in Preemption

For Claudius Lysias, who stopped a notable preemption-murder; and for all others like him.

CHAPTER 1

It was not a difficult decision, in the end. But it would have to be carefully executed so that she did not suspect.

Kathleen Doyle was walking with her husband on the grounds of Trestles, his hereditary estate. She was recovering from a concussion she'd sustained when she fell from a collapsed balcony in London—was fully recovered, as a matter of fact, although Acton, her husband, tended to be a worry-wart when it came to her; so much so that he'd been turning aside any discussion of when they could return to their London flat, which was home base for them.

And Trestles might be the perfect place to recover from her injuries in peace and quiet, but it was also the perfect place to hold someone prisoner in that it was built in medieval times when such things tended to happen as a matter of course. Therefore—unless she made an attempt to scale over the walls at night—Doyle stood little chance of escape. And even scaling the walls wouldn't be a workable solution, being as the gamekeeper had an obnoxious dog who always seemed to know where she was—she'd never make it as far as the kitchen garden.

Added to this problem was another, more pressing one; the lord and master of this place—who walked beside her, at present—was a bit mad. There was no bunkin' this home-truth, and you need only look to her current circumstances for confirmation. The dire events of the balcony-collapse had thrown him, and he was one who didn't like being thrown—probably because he was so unused to it. And although she'd been conked-out for a couple of days, she was fairly certain that he'd left a trail of mayhem in London—Acton was not one who would take kindly to an attack on his wedded wife.

He'd already admitted that the two people most responsible for her injuries were no longer alive, and she'd the sure sense there was much he wasn't telling her. Something had happened, and whatever-it-was was a doozy; she'd been whisked off to Trestles, people were dead, and—most improbable of all—someone had given her husband a black eye. It was almost completely healed now, but the fact that anyone had got close enough to do such a thing was a marvel in and of itself; Acton was a Chief Inspector at Scotland Yard, after all.

And the fact that he was carefully keeping her in the dark only strengthened her suspicion that she'd best shake her stumps and find out what had happened whilst she was out-for-the-count. Whatever it was, the fall-out was such that he'd locked her away here—which was rather alarming, as they'd experienced many a perilous adventure together without his feeling that she should be removed from the arena of operations.

Doyle loved her husband—loved him fiercely—but she'd been a bit daunted to find out, early in their marriage, that he wasn't at all what he appeared to be in the eyes of his admiring public. They'd been paired-up when she was a rookie detective

—it was an odd partnering, in that she was something of a naïve bumbler whilst he was a much-admired solver-of-crimes; he was known to be brilliant and reclusive, and not one to suffer fools.

Little did she know, at the time, that he'd arranged to enlist her as his support officer so that he could coax her into marriage—which he did, smooth-as-silk, and with nary a hint of what was in the offing. No one had been aware that the illustrious Chief Inspector had fallen hard for the unlikely Doyle—least of all Doyle, herself—nor were they aware of the depths of his devotion to his Irish bride. It was actually the first hint she'd had that his mind was a bit off-kilter; he'd seen her from his office window, walking on the pavement down below, and had immediately embarked on a campaign to buckle her up.

And perhaps Doyle was a bit mad too, because she'd been willing to marry the man at the drop of a hat, so to speak. She admired him of course—everyone did—but that didn't explain why she'd jumped over the traces in such an unexpected way; up to that point, she'd been rather shy—and with good reason. Doyle was what the Irish would call "fey," which meant that she was extremely perceptive when it came to other people and could read their emotions, even when they were quite good at hiding those emotions. It was a useful talent in detective-work—especially because she could usually tell when someone was lying.

It was a double-edged sword, though; whilst it meant she could sift through lies and untruths when she heard them, it also meant she'd spent much of her life avoiding other people—it was no easy thing, to be battered by cross-currents of emotion everywhere you went.

But despite this, she'd not raised a finger of objection when Acton had suggested they marry on the same day that he proposed. Or perhaps it was because of it; at the time, Acton was the only person on earth who knew about her perceptive abilities—strangely enough, she'd told him about it the first case they'd worked together. The very same instinct that made her shy away from others told her that she could trust him completely, and trust him she did—even after discovering there was good reason for Acton to insist on a whirlwind wedding; in the same way that she was not at all what she seemed, he was not at all what he seemed, either.

Acton had a dark side—which was putting it rather mildly—and it tended to manifest itself when he was stymied by the safeguards that were put in place to protect the criminal class. If the justice system allowed a villain to go free, Acton would see to it that the villain paid a price nevertheless, and with no one the wiser. He acted as judge and jury and would dispense justice as he saw fit with little consideration for the laws of the land.

Doyle's acute dismay at discovering her husband's vigilante tendencies had caused him to temper his actions somewhat—he lived to please her, after all—but she'd not been completely successful in curbing his wayward ways; he was an aristocrat with a thousand years of iron-fisted rule at his back, and thus saw no problem in sorting-out the villains and smiting whichever enemies were foolish enough to cross him. Not that the public was aware of any of this; Acton was the grand-master at covering his tracks.

Nonetheless, over the course of her unexpected marriage—which now included two young boys as well as a daughter on the way—Doyle liked to think that she'd coaxed her volatile husband onto a better path. He was definitely not as self-destructive as he'd been before he'd married her and—as a hopeful symptom of this—he tended to sink into his black moods on fewer and fewer occasions. The black moods were fearsome to behold in that his inner demons—which were many and persistent, poor man—would rear their nasty heads, and he'd shutter himself within himself, to drink and to brood.

Truth to tell, it was something of a miracle that Doyle's latest brush with disaster hadn't inspired the mother of all black moods. She'd been investigating a money-laundering enterprise that was operating out of a London marina—artwork was being traded at inflated prices so as to disguise illicit profits from various criminal enterprises. As the CID was closing-in on a take-down, the villains had panicked and set the marina afire, with the fair Doyle having been forced to leap from a fiery balcony into the Thames, where she'd been knocked unconscious and had to be fished-out.

Therefore, in light of her adventures in getting conked-on-the-head, you'd think that Acton's demons would be rearing-up to beat the band but instead, he'd been surprisingly calm these last ten days and seemingly content to spend a peaceful holiday here with their boys.

Something's up, she thought, and not for the first time; Acton's not a mild-as-milk sort of person and I'd best find out why he's gone off-script—something's brewing, and it's brewing big.

But this resolve created something of a dilemma, since at the present time she was locked away in a place that hadn't seen fit to change since the seventeenth-century alongside a husband who was equally strong-minded. Fortunately, his strength-of-mind was often overcome by his willingness to please his wife, and so at least she'd that card to pull.

Making an attempt at subtlety—never her strong suit—Doyle began in an admiring tone, "It's truly beautiful here, isn't it? With the sunlight, comin' in through the trees?"

This was the surest way to soften him up; Acton loved this place in a way that an Irish shant like Doyle couldn't truly comprehend—instead, she'd mixed-emotions about Trestles and the whole rule-by-might mindset that had created it. But the place was indeed lovely; she always felt as though time stood still, whenever they visited.

"It is," he agreed.

"The boyos love to climb the trees—and the pond's gettin' a workout; I imagine it hasn't seen this much splashin' in a century or two."

Her husband drew her to him with a fond arm. "What is it you would like to ask me, Kathleen?"

He'd seen right through her attempt to soften him up, of course—she always had the sneaking suspicion that he knew her better than she knew herself—and so she decided to cut to the nub. "Sooner or later, you're goin' to have to tell me what's happened, Michael—for heaven's sake."

He considered this, as he raised his gaze to contemplate the spreading branches overhead. "I do not believe that I do."

"I'm excellent at winklin'-out things," she reminded him. "None better."

"Very true," he agreed, and offered nothing more.

As they continued to walk along, arm-in-arm, she persisted, "Are we goin' back home, anytime soon?"

"Perhaps not for the near future. You must rest, and think of little Mary."

Mary was their unborn daughter, who was too tiny to care about whatever hair-raising adventures her mother may have experienced and so Doyle recognized a hedge when she heard it. "I'm *fine*, Michael—my hand on my heart—and nowhere near as fragile as you seem to think. I'm not cut out to be idle-rich, and all this coddlin' is drivin' me mad."

"Allow me to be the judge of this, please."

Since this was said with a level of firmness that was unusual for him when dealing with her, she decided to try a different tack. "The villains are goin' to run amok if you're not loomin' large, Michael. You should be out there reelin' 'em in, now that they're set back on their heels."

This was a valid point, in that the artwork money-laundering scheme was extensive and involved both sides of the channel. Now that it was apparent the rig was in the crosshairs of the CID, the kingpins behind it were frantically destroying all evidence and snuffing-out anyone who could possibly testify against them. Preemption-murders, the CID called them; the big fish were targeting the little fish so as to protect themselves, with law enforcement having little incentive to intervene.

And in the usual course of things, Doyle's husband would be frenetically busy, monitoring the collapse of such an extensive scheme and scooping-up whoever was left standing, but instead here they were—being all tranquil and such. Which only made it all the more puzzling; Acton tended to handle the Met's most high-profile cases—being as his was a good face to put in front of the public—and therefore his absence would be keenly felt.

His answer, however, was completely unexpected. "Unfortunately, I have been placed on administrative leave."

She halted mid-stride to stare at him, shocked to the core. "*Holy* Mother of God, Michael—what's happened? You must have truly cocked-up, if they're willin' to put the likes of you on leave."

He tilted his head. "A misunderstanding, only. After an investigation, I expect to be fully reinstated."

"Have I been put on leave, too?" she ventured. This might explain her husband's out-sized desire to keep her in the dark.

"No," he replied, amused as he gently took her elbow and steered her forward. "Instead, the Met has received an outpouring of support and good wishes."

She couldn't help but laugh at the irony. "Fancy that; it's my reputation that's goin' to pull you out of the coals, for a change." Doyle was much-loved by the public in that she'd received two commendations for bravery and the news media had made much of it, being as she was female and they were heartily sick of the male officers always being the brave ones.

"One would hope. But I am certain that once the process concludes, I will be exonerated."

"Exonerated from what?" she ventured.

"A mere misunderstanding," he advised again, in a patented Acton non-answer.

She took an educated guess. "Does this 'misunderstandin'' have anythin' to do with Denisovich and Elliott gettin' themselves killed?"

Igor Denisovich and Walter Elliott were the two players in the artwork-rig who'd been most responsible for her ordeal on that disaster-day, and the two had been found murdered in short order—their murders having all the earmarks of a professional hit.

"Not at all; the working-theory is that theirs are preemption-murders."

She made a wry mouth, because she would bet her teeth that these two had actually died at the hands of her vengeful husband. He'd have been furious, of course—not to mention that this was his usual m.o.; Acton loved nothing more than to set the villains against themselves, and then stand idly by whilst they annihilated one another, hammer and tongs.

She eyed him sidelong as they walked along. "Why's everythin' so shrouded in secrecy, my friend? You're makin' me very uneasy, and I can't think that's good for my poor noggin."

Apparently deciding that he had to give her a more palatable answer, he offered, "I would like to give it some time and distance, before we return."

This was understandable, if he'd misbehaved to the extent that he'd been placed on leave. She squeezed his waist in sympathy—he would have hated the feeling of helplessness, upon discovering that she was in terrible danger and there was no immediate remedy. Small wonder there was scorched-earth back in London—although it remained to be seen exactly how scorched.

Which once again seemed to contradict his current mood; he seemed calm as a nun's cat, and in no hurry to take-up the reins again. He's allowing the pot to stir itself, she decided; the villains are turning on each other, the dominos are falling, and he knows better than to interfere. Acton could swing a sword with the best of them but he could also be very, very patient when the occasion warranted.

Hoping for a bit more insight, she teased, "Well, God's havin' a good laugh, Michael. If ever there was a fine lesson that you're not always able to control things, there it was when I wound-up in the stupid river yet again. You must have been fit to be tied."

"Indeed," he replied. "Shall we return for luncheon? You must not over-exert yourself."

Doesn't want to talk about it, she thought; and small blame to him. I'd like to hear the tale—being as I missed out on much of it—but apparently the memory is still a bit too fresh for the poor man. Which also means he's not going to give me any hints about why we wound-up here instead of our London flat, and why he's been suspended—although I'll bet a draper's purse it has something to do with his black eye.

"Foine," she replied in her broadest accent, which was how she tended to tease him whenever he lapsed into aristo-speak. "Is Grady makin' lunch?" The place was operating on a skeleton-staff at present, with the Irish gamekeeper being—apparently—one of the few personnel Acton felt he could trust.

"Grady is making pasties," he affirmed.

She brightened, since this was a favorite treat from her childhood—lard-laden pasties, hot from the vendor's cart on the Dublin docks; Grady had a similar recipe he'd cribbed from his gran. "Well then, let's eat; I may be under lock-and-key, but as least I've a kindly warden."

CHAPTER 2

He'd little choice but to see it through. Regrettable, but necessary.

That night, Doyle had one of her dreams.

She had them, on occasion; dreams which truly didn't seem like dreams because they were so vivid, even though they tended to be hard to describe—all impressions and darkness, with the sound of wind blowing all around her even though she couldn't feel it against her skin. Bewildering dreams, that didn't seem tethered in any way to reality—save that they always featured a very real-seeming ghost.

The dreams were a more recent manifestation of Doyle's perceptive abilities—or at least, she'd never had them prior to marrying Acton and that didn't seem a coincidence. In these dreams, the ghost was sometimes attempting to relay a warning about a coming catastrophe—the catastrophe being the direct result of some plot that Acton was cooking-up on the sly—and sometimes, by contrast, the warning sought to enlist Acton's help to prevent a catastrophe with the fair Doyle serving as the early-warning system. And then again, there was the occasional dream where the ghost was an evil one, and trying to trick the fair Doyle into her own catastrophe.

In fact, she'd been served just such a trick by the last ghost she'd encountered and so she was understandably wary when it came to facing the next one. However, she decided—with a huge sense of relief—that it was probably no coincidence the ghost who stood before her was someone she felt she could solidly trust.

"Hallo, Mr. Maguire," she said.

"Hallo, Officer Doyle," the ghost answered in a genial tone.

Kevin Maguire had been a journalist with the *London World Times* and they'd become friends-of-sorts, even though he'd been intent on publishing an exposé about Acton's many misdeeds—he was one of the few people who was aware of how Acton actually operated, behind his public facade. The reporter had spiked his story, however, due to his friendship with Doyle—not to mention he was largely responsible for her status as a heroic figure, being as he'd greatly sensationalized her adventures in police-work.

There was a small silence, and Doyle ventured, "I need to find out what's happened. It must be a corker, if we've retreated here and drawn-up the drawbridge."

Maguire replied, "No one knows what happened except your husband."

She blinked. "That's a bit hard to believe, Mr. Maguire; there were a lot of people involved in the marina-fire. Not to mention the CID was about to charge in and arrest the lot—they've been tryin' to put together a case for a donkey's age."

"Very true," he agreed.

Since his response didn't seem to make much sense, she persisted, "Denisovich and Elliott were killed almost before the fire was put out, and Acton says the workin'-theory is that theirs were preemption-murders. I'd be very much shocked, though, if it wasn't Acton himself who's killed them—I've that feelin'. And it only stands to reason, because he's done such a thing before—made it seem as though the villains were killin' each other in a panic, so as to set them against each other." She paused, and then added with grudging admiration, "No one knows how to stir-up a panic better than Acton."

But the ghost only cautioned, "Follow the story, Officer Doyle. It is important to make certain you have your facts straight."

This was unexpected, particularly because if she didn't know better it sounded as though Maguire was defending Acton—which would truly be a turnaround; Maguire was not an admirer of aristocrats who went about doing whatever they wished. Not to mention that she knew—knew down to the soles of her shoes—that Acton had indeed executed both men. After all, Igor Denisovich and Walter Elliott had been most responsible for her ordeal, and Doyle's husband wasn't one to hesitate in bringing down the hammer when it came to bloody vengeance. The fact that it would have the added benefit of pitting all the other foot-soldiers against each other would only be the icing on the cake.

And it was all rather ironic, because—whilst the two dead men had indeed played a role in that disaster-day—the main driver had been an evil ghost, bent on her own vengeance. No one knew this save Doyle, of course—but surely, the present ghost would be well-aware?

In some confusion, she ventured, "I'm not sure there's much of a story to unearth, Mr. Maguire; it all seems very straightforward. Faith, we're lucky Acton didn't wipe-out half the villains in London."

But the ghost only reiterated, "You must find out exactly what happened. In news work, it is important to gather-up all the facts before going to press."

Fairly, she nodded. "Aye—that's how police work is, too. You're supposed to follow the evidence, and be willin' to abandon your workin'-theory if the evidence doesn't support it."

"Very similar," he agreed.

Another small silence ensued, and she ventured, "I don't know, Mr. Maguire; this has Acton's fingerprints all over it."

"Yes," the ghost agreed. "All tracks neatly covered; all problems neatly eliminated."

This seemed to hint that there was more going on here than met the eye, but she pointed out in a practical manner, "Even if there is more to the story—as you seem to think—I don't know how I'm goin' to find out a blessed thing; he's buttoned-up and not budgin'."

"If one source of information is closed off, then you must find another."

She raised her palms. "I'm not sure what you want me to do, though; I'm on disability leave, and so I can't put on my detective-hat and wander about askin' questions." Sobering, she added, "Besides, I've got to tread carefully; he hates it when I get hurt—and he doubly hates it when he's not able to control things. It must be chafin' him no end."

The ghost tilted his head. "Does he seem chafed?"

After a pause, she admitted, "No, not that anyone can see. But I've the sense that beneath it all, he's—he's unhappy, and on edge." She nodded, thinking about this. "He's waitin' for the trumpet to sound, even though he doesn't want to go to war."

"Yes," Maguire agreed. "Very apt."

Doyle knit her brow. "So; he's waitin' and calm—not

unhappy about bein' suspended—and he seems to think it will all be cleared-up very soon. Which is probably the case—Professional Standards has to step carefully; whatever he's done, they can't come down too hard because the public loves him. Loves me, too."

Suddenly struck with an unwelcome thought, she lifted her startled gaze to his. "Mother a' *Mercy;* I hope they're not goin' to give me another commendation."

The ghost chuckled. "No—instead it is Rolph Denisovich, who will be given an award by the Lord Mayor."

Doyle laughed aloud. "Is that so? Faith, 'tis the eighth wonder of the world—who'd have thought?"

Rolph Denisovich—the late Igor Denisovich's nephew—was a young man who'd heretofore been something of a ne'er-do-well but who—rather surprisingly—had come to the fair Doyle's rescue in this latest misadventure.

Thinking about this, she shook her head in wonder. "We're truly livin' in upside-down world, if Rolph's the hero and Acton's been suspended. A true reversion—reversion of—"

"Reversal of fortune," he supplied. "Or so it would seem."

His last words hung in the air, and she regarded him with some puzzlement. "Oh? So; everything's not how it looks? Faith, why can't any of you lot just *tell me*, straight out?"

"Because you must piece it together for yourself; you must follow the story." He paused. "It's important."

"It always is," she groused. "But you're forgettin' that I'm thick as a plank."

The ghost offered in an encouraging tone, "Don't sell yourself short, Officer Doyle; you are very resourceful when you need to be."

Perplexed, Doyle raised her palms again. "I don't know what you expect me to do, Mr. Maguire—I've been sidelined. And anyways, I don't dare tell him that it was actually a nasty ghost who's caused all this ruckus."

"True," he agreed. "That wouldn't help matters at all—in fact, may even make them worse."

"Aye—he'd lock me away in the garret, sure as the sun rises."

"I believe—" the ghost pointed out with some delicacy, "—that this has already occurred."

There was another small silence as Doyle contemplated this rather unwelcome truth. "Oh. So, you're sayin' I need to bust out."

"You're not so very helpless," her companion urged. "In fact, you're one of the bravest people I know."

She made a wry mouth. "You're believin' your own articles, Mr. Maguire. And besides, I truly have to step carefully because I'm not sure what's happened, and I don't want to make everythin' worse. Faith, you need only to look at Acton's suspension; he's done plenty of things in the past that *should* have got him suspended but whatever's happened, he's finally been called on the carpet—which only goes to show that it must have been a corker."

"Follow the story," the newsman repeated. "You're a police officer and a hero, don't forget; it gives you access."

"Oh," she realized, as the penny dropped. *"That's* why you've shown up; I should go over to the *London World News* and find out what's happened from the people who are most likely to know."

"There you go," he agreed with a satisfied smile.

With amused exasperation, she asked, "Well, why didn't you just *say* so? Not to mention it seems very strange, that you're comin' forward to help Acton. That's a bit of a corker, in and of itself."

The ghost admitted, "It's more along the lines that I'm doing a favor for a friend."

"Oh. All right, then—so long as you're not leadin' me into a trap. Are you?" After her last ghostly experience, she was a bit leery.

"No," Maguire replied. "I'm not the trap-setter, here."

CHAPTER 3

There remained a small lump on her head where the injury had been. He hoped it wasn't permanent.

The following morning, Doyle was at the breakfast table with her two little boys as they finished-up their morning meal. Trestles had a breakfast room—it was considered an informal nook, even though it was the size of Doyle's entire flat, growing up—and she idly watched the boys tear into yet another slice of toast-and-jam as the faint sounds of a piano could be heard in the distance.

Acton had finished his breakfast and then excused himself so that he could retreat to his piano for an hour or so, which was his usual routine these mornings. She could hear the strains of the music from the floor above them—some complicated classical tune that didn't lend itself to whistling—and decided that she'd been indeed fuzzy-minded not to have realized that the man was scheming-up some scheme that was certain to turn her red hair grey.

Acton played when he was deep in thought, and so the odds were good that he was masterminding some way out of his current circumstance—which would also explain the absence of any black moods. As she'd said to Maguire, it seemed that he was waiting to hear the trumpet sound—and Katy bar the door, because she'd the sense that whatever it would mean, it was a bone-rattler. At least he hadn't taken-up smoking again—thank the saints for small favors.

She frowned a bit as she listened, because she'd the sense that her husband was unhappy—even though the music wasn't sad-sounding music. Not that he was necessarily *sad*, it was more as though he was—*unsettled*, mayhap was the right word. Unsettled, and on edge—waiting to hear that trumpet.

Which was interesting; Maguire had made it sound as though Acton was in the process of setting a trap—which would be miles more in keeping for the man, truth to tell, than the idea that he'd retreat to Trestles to lick his wounds. But Doyle—who'd plenty of experience with her husband when he was in trap-setting mode—didn't see any signs of such, mainly because you'd think he'd be eager to be back in London if such were the case—back in London and monitoring the panic that would be spreading amongst the underworld like ripples on a pond.

But instead here he was, seemingly content to respect the terms of his suspension and await events. It was all very strange, and since Maguire was urging her to find out exactly what had happened during the time that she was out-for-the-count, she'd best gird her loins and get on with it.

"Another slice, ma'am?"

Doyle offered-up a smile. "I will, thank you Grady. And I hate to heap more burdens atop your others, but I was thinkin' the boys might like to go horseback ridin' again."

"Happy to oblige, ma'am. When were you thinkin'?"

In a casual tone, she replied, "No rush—I know you've double-duties. And we've got nothin' a'tall planned for today."

"Shall we say in an hour? That should give me enough time to get the ponies tacked-out."

"Grand." She eyed him. "How's that dog o' yours?"

"Never you fear, ma'am; I'll put Laddie up in my rooms so's he won't fash at you."

"Well, I suppose no one can blame the beast for thinkin' I'm an intruder, here—I feel the same way, myself."

He chuckled—just as she'd intended—and offered, "He did love his swim, yesterday; never seen him so tired."

Edward, Doyle's eldest, had discovered that the dog would dash madly into the pond to fetch a stick and so this noisy pastime had taken up most of the afternoon.

"Edward, too," Doyle agreed. "I don't know who was the more spent between the two, and it's the very reason I'm lookin' to go ridin' today—somethin' a bit more restful is called-for."

After Grady left for the stables, Doyle led her boys into the manor house's main foyer—a stately room with high ceilings and hammer-beams in the best English-nob tradition. There were ghosts about, of course—Trestles was the only place she saw ghosts outside of her dreams, and there were always piles of them huddled amongst the rafters, watching her with great interest. She ignored them as best she could—it was one of the reasons she wasn't so very fond of this place; the ever-present ghosts were that annoying.

She dallied in the sunlit foyer, letting the boys jump along the square marble tiles, vying with each other to see how many squares they could jump. And as could be expected, Hudson—Trestles' steward—soon made an appearance, pausing discreetly in the doorway that led into the drawing room.

Hudson was an elderly man—very correct—and just the

type of retainer who would discreetly show himself if the lady of the house was dallying somewhere, in the event that she might require his assistance. Not to mention that the master of the house had no doubt tasked the steward with keeping an eye on the man's wedded wife whilst he was busy playing the piano and scheming-up unhappy schemes.

"Ho, Hudson," Doyle addressed the steward in a cheerful tone. "I've a task for you."

"Certainly, madam," the man replied, as he inclined his head to precisely the correct degree.

"You're goin' to have to lock Acton in his music room and have the car brought 'round." She paused, thinking about his. "Make sure to put in the car seats."

It was a testament to his deportment that Hudson didn't blink an eyelash at this request. "Very good, madam. Am I to understand you are leaving?"

"I am. I'm goin' to bust out, and you're goin' to be an aider-and-abettor else I'll tell Acton you were cross with me, and he'll sack you without a moment's hesitation."

"Certainly, madam. If I might suggest—"

"Ah-ah," she warned, holding up a finger to cut him off. "Just get it done, please."

She then waited with the boys, who'd tired of their jumping game and instead decided to bang on the suits of armor that were on display in the foyer, much to the dismay of the ghost-knights who'd worn them.

Acton soon appeared and came over to kiss her in greeting. "I understand you are enlisting Hudson to escape."

As he drew her into his arms, she admitted, "I am. Faith, the wretched man grassed me out."

He dropped a kiss on the top of her head. "We will go home, then."

Since she knew he was suffering from mixed emotions, she lifted her face to assure him, "It will be all right, Michael—we've got to go back sometime. And if you're in hot water, the best strategy is to face the music and humbly apologize for any wrongs that were wrung. A contrite heart goes a long way."

"Very well."

She made a sound of sympathy, since he wouldn't have the least idea how to go about having a contrite heart. "It's not 'very well' a'tall, but we'll muddle through; no need to sound the retreat. And anyways, this place wouldn't be able to withstand the boys for much longer—poor Hudson has aged ten years."

Hudson offered a small, dry smile at this sally but Doyle could sense that the steward was relieved; aside from Doyle, he was probably the person best able to assess Acton's moods and so he must have been a bit concerned—it was very unlike Acton to be placidly idle for any stretch of time.

No, she thought, as she met Hudson's gaze with her own discreet, reassuring one; it is very unlike Acton to be content to hide-away and I was definitely off my game not to have realized it before a ghost had to show up to remind me. There's a trap being set, and I've the weighty task of finding out for who—whom?—it's being set, before it gets sprung. Apparently, it's important.

CHAPTER 4

Perhaps he'd install a piano in the London flat.

Doyle decided that the car-ride back to town would serve as an excellent opportunity to do a bit of subtle probing, and with this in mind she waited until the boys were asleep—nothing like a car ride after a bit of armor-knocking to put them out—and then she casually remarked, "What are you up to, husband?" Let it again be said that subtlety was not her strong suit.

To his credit, he made no disclaimer—he was as well-used to her ways as she was to his—but only said again, "I thought it would be best to give the situation some time and distance."

"Fair enough," she replied. "As long as you weren't plannin' to lock me up in the garret, like the first wife in that famous story about the governess."

He smiled slightly. "Perish the thought."

"Oh, you'd do it, if you thought I'd stand for it."

He took her hand. "No. Upon my honor."

"Well, that tears it, then; your honor is mighty hit-and-miss."

"Not when it comes to you," he insisted. "I am sorry, Kathleen. Perhaps I overreacted."

She gave him a sidelong glance. "What, exactly, did you over-react to?"

There was a small pause. "I was unhappy with the quality of care at the hospital, and so I enlisted McGonigal and brought you to Trestles at the first opportunity."

This rang true, and she nodded, since this much seemed apparent. "Poor Tim; he's always on-call for the latest catastrophe."

Tim McGonigal was Acton's friend from university days; loyal and discreet, the doctor had been summoned on many an occasion to offer medical care when the occasion warranted. He'd been at Trestles for those first few days after she'd regained consciousness, and then he'd come back several times to check on her.

Since her husband had been willing to offer this much, Doyle decided there was no time like the present to cut to the nub. "So; who gave you the shiner?"

He thought about it for a moment and then replied, "I'd rather not say."

She raised her brows. "Why's it such a mystery?"

"Because events are still pending."

With a sigh, she turned to gaze out her window, unsurprised. "Well, of all the mysterious goings-on that I missed out on, that one takes the palm. Not to mention there's not a lot of people you'd allow close enough to give you a black eye, Michael—you should have fobbed me off by claimin' you'd walked into a gate, or somethin'."

"You would know that such a claim was not the truth."

"Aye," she acknowledged. "I suppose that does cut down on the husbandly flim-flam."

His tone very serious, he squeezed the hand he held in his. "I'm afraid you must trust me, Kathleen. Believe me when I say it is for the best that you know as little as possible."

She skewed her gaze back to him. "Wouldn't that be for me to decide?"

"No," he said bluntly. "Oftentimes, your judgement is a bit naïve."

This was of interest, in that it indicated he'd put a tight lid on the aforesaid goings-on because she was a weak-link—although to be fair, compared to him everyone was a weak-link. How ironic, that the poor man's life was miles more complicated, all because he'd allowed this particular weak-link into his carefully-ordered world.

Her scalp prickled—which was what it did when her intuition was prodding her to pay attention—and she frowned slightly. Acton had gone on scramble-drill for unknown reasons, but didn't want her to know the details because she might blunder-about and ruin his plans. He was setting a trap, according to Maguire—even though the two main villains were dead, he'd been suspended from the CID and—lest we forget—he'd come out the worse in a fistfight. Faith, it was all very through-the-looking-glass and she wouldn't be half-surprised to discover she was still delirious from her knock on the noggin.

I won't press him, she decided, as she reviewed the passing scenery. Instead, I'll do as Maguire suggests and go for a nose-about at the *London World News*. There's a piece to this puzzle that I'm missing, and apparently that's the best place to start—even though that doesn't make a lot of sense, being as Maguire himself said that no one knew what happened save Acton.

Whilst she was puzzling over this apparent contradiction,

her husband asked, "How did you find your stay at Trestles? Were there as many ghosts, this time?"

This was surprising, in that Acton didn't like to bring up her ghost-sightings. He would listen if she spoke of it—and he was well-aware that the aforesaid ghosts had been helpful on more than one occasion—but he never broached the subject on his own, being as he was half-convinced she was barkin' mad.

"The usual suspects," she advised him in a vague tone, being as she didn't much like to speak of it, either. And there was definitely no need to mention that the ranking knight-in-residence was sorely annoyed that Edward didn't have his own sword as yet. Faith, Acton would probably think it an excellent idea, so all the more reason not to say.

She could sense her husband's quick flare of disappointment, even though he'd listened to her response with an impassive expression. It was a bit surprising—mayhap he'd been hoping that her conk-on-the-head had cured her of such fancies. Small chance of that, though; she may be naïve and thick as a plank, but even she could see that it was no coincidence she'd started having these ghost-dreams shortly after she'd married a powerful man who—despite being sworn law enforcement—was a ruthless vigilante, behind the scenes. It seemed apparent that she'd been tasked with being some sort of link between two worlds, and was left to make the best of it.

Hard on this thought, he squeezed her hand again and said almost gently, "You know that you must never speak of it—of your abilities—to anyone."

This was a continuing concern for him, since he knew she'd a tendency to gabble—it was that whole weak-link thing. "I know, Michael. Although even if I did, no one would believe it—they would just think me mad."

"It would be much worse if you were indeed believed."

To reassure him, she lifted his hand to kiss its back. "I know, Michael—I've been very careful my whole life long; not to worry."

They'd been over this ground many a time before, mainly because she'd once told Thomas Williams—her best friend and a fellow-detective—about her truth-detecting abilities, and Acton had been very unhappy about it. But it had been important at the time—Williams was heading for a disaster, and she'd had to warn him off.

Nonetheless, her husband had advised her, very seriously, that if her perceptive abilities were ever made known there was a huge danger that she'd be snatched-up by the shadowy intelligence agencies, and forced into their rather ruthless service.

And—as it turned out—his warning was spot-on, because an MI 5 supervisor had indeed conducted an experiment to see if any rank-and-file Met employees might have extra-sensory abilities that would be useful in their spy-business. At Acton's urging, Doyle had carefully faked her answers so that no suspicions would be raised, and that particular crisis had been thankfully averted. Although the MI 5 supervisor had gone missing shortly afterward, poor thing; hers was a dangerous business.

Her husband's voice interrupted her thoughts. "I would ask that you not go back to work until you are cleared by McGonigal."

She eyed him sidelong yet again, because Tim McGonigal was going to do whatever Acton told him to. "And when's that, my friend?"

"Perhaps we will wait until I have been reinstated."

She couldn't argue the point, because this only made sense—it would be awkward beyond measure if Acton's wife had to parry a bunch of questions about his suspension—especially since her wedded husband seemed to be concerned that she might actually find out what had happened.

"Right, then. As long as you're not plannin' on lockin' me away in the London flat, as opposed to the garret at Trestles."

"As to that," he admitted, "I might make mention that I've purchased the flat below ours—just so that we'd have extra space." This, because he knew that the wife of his bosom would not be best-pleased about this purchase; she was not one to be comfortable living in a luxury two-story flat, let alone a luxury three-story one.

She made a wry mouth. "That's mighty expensive extra space, Michael."

"If we moved my office to the lower level, it would allow each of the children to have their own room on the second floor," he reasoned. "And I would appreciate the additional work-space."

She nodded in resignation, since she'd known he'd been champing to buy-up the additional floor will-she or nil-she; Acton didn't like having people underfoot, and so it stood to reason that he'd want an entire floor to himself. "Aye, then. So long as you're not goin' to be meetin' with your mistress down there—faith, it *is* like that story with the governess, with you tryin' to juggle the both of us 'neath the same roof."

He smiled. "I do not have a mistress."

"Truly?" she asked in feigned surprise. "Are you takin' up Holy Orders, instead?"

There was a small pause. "Am I to understand that you are feeling neglected?"

"You are indeed 'to understand', husband—you're avoidin' me like I'm a wizened-up alewife." During her recovery he'd been reluctant to have sex, the knocker—although to be fair, their bed-sport did tend to be a bit vigorous, with the occasional bruise courtesy of the headboard.

"I will endeavor to make amends," he promised, amused.

"Aye, you will. Best roll-up your sleeves and get on with the endeavorin' else it will be me who installs a—a—" She knit her brow. "What's the male equivalent of a mistress?"

"A paramour," he supplied.

She looked at him in surprise. "*Paramour*? That's the word?"

"Paramour," he affirmed.

She made a sound of derision, and turned to face her window again. "Faith, a 'paramour' doesn't sound like someone any female worth her salt would want to have sex with. They should come up with a better word."

"Indeed."

"It's not *funny*, Michael; you only laugh because your word is so much better. 'Mistress' brings to mind a beautiful goddess-in-charge, whilst a paraman—"

"Paramour."

"—paramour sounds like a wimpy little half-man."

"Perhaps the language could be improved," he suggested diplomatically.

She nodded. "Aye, and that's why God invented Gaelic, my friend; '*stócach*' sounds exactly like someone a woman would want to take to bed."

"Very hard to argue," Acton agreed.

CHAPTER 5

A shame, that they could not remain at Trestles for a few more days.

It felt good to be home at the London flat again, and back to normal—as normal as could be expected, of course, what with the two boys racing about in their excitement and whatever-Acton-was-brewing looming large.

Doyle greeted Reynolds, their butler, who did not reveal by the turn of a hair that he thought recent events were in any way unusual; it was very similar to Hudson's poker-face, and they must teach it to them on the first day of servant-school. But since Doyle was not a discreet sort of person, she told him in a cheerful tone, "Thank God fastin' we're back, Reynolds; Acton had me locked-away and I was half-thinkin' I'd have to send you a message by carrier pigeon, askin' you to come by and bring a grapplin' hook."

"I am gratified such a course wasn't necessary, madam," the butler replied in a neutral tone, since—although he and Doyle shared a deep affection—the butler knew upon which side his bread was buttered.

"Well, Acton was worried my brains had got addled but I think it's too hard for him to tell, and so he threw in the towel and here we are."

"You are feeling well, madam?"

"I am. As a matter of fact, I think I'll go shoppin' later today."

Doyle had laid the groundwork for today's excursion by telling Acton that she needed a new pair of spike-heeled black boots so as to lure him into bed—which was nonsense, of course, in that her old pair had turned the trick just fine. And he was better for it—she could tell. A return to normal was exactly what was needed, and Doyle congratulated herself for getting him away from his brooding-piano and back into the marital bed, which was miles more efficient at easing his mind.

Not that she was home free, of course; she could sense he was uneasy about having her back here in the thick of things, and mayhap discovering whatever-it-was that he didn't want her to find out. But the poor man's fretting was all in vain; she could say with all modesty that she'd an excellent record of throwing a spanner into Acton's wheel-of-many-works, and so off to the *London World News* she would go. Interesting, that the ghost this time around was Kevin Maguire; usually the identity of the ghost turned out to be important, in some way.

"Shall I accompany you, madam?"

Recalled from her abstraction, Doyle told the butler, "No thanks; mainly I'm just wantin' to have a walk-about and listen to the city. You don't realize how much you miss the bustle; peacefulness is grossly overrated, and don't let anyone tell you otherwise."

"Lord Acton is aware of your intention, madam?"

"He is," she affirmed, and thought it interesting that Reynolds must had been given the head's up not to let her wander off under her own devices. "Trenton will come along, of course. And I'm goin' to meet Lizzie Williams for tea."

Trenton was their security-man, and Lizzie Williams worked in the forensics lab at the CID. The young woman had been strategically placed there by Acton himself, because she hailed from Trestles and tended to be an accessory to whatever questionable scheme he had in play—very convenient to have a forensic scientist on hand when one needed to skew the evidence a bit.

Lizzie also happened to be married to Doyle's best friend, Thomas Williams, but Lizzie wasn't much in the way of a boon companion herself, mainly because she was dry and intelligent and therefore the mirror-opposite of Doyle. This time around, however, the tables would be turned and Doyle was hoping—for once—to get one over on Lizzie, if all went according to plan.

As he considered the day's schedule, the butler asked, "Will you be home in time to fetch Master Edward from St. Margaret's, madam, or shall I?"

"I will. And as a matter of fact, Acton wants to walk over to school with us this mornin', since he's at loose-ends and is lookin' for somethin' useful to do. Mayhap you could give him some silver to polish."

As could be expected, the butler ignored this irreverent remark and instead returned to the kitchen to pack Edward's lunch.

Watching him, Doyle idly considered the interesting fact that Reynolds had said nothing upon seeing Acton's shiner when he'd greeted their arrival yesterday. Over the past ten days, the black eye had faded to a yellow-tinged bruise but it was nonetheless still visible. Which meant that either Reynolds had weighed the situation and decided not to offer any remark—after all, the man's wedded wife might have hauled off and hit him with a joint-stool—or Reynolds already knew what had happened. And she'd the sense, for some reason, that this was indeed the case; the butler was aware of what had happened and was carefully making no comment.

Doyle frowned slightly, because her husband's injury seemed significant to her; who could have got close enough to Acton to belt him one, without his thwarting a frontal attack? It seemed a small universe of suspects; she would top the list, of course, and it was possible that she may have socked him all unknowing—it was unclear how much of a struggle it had been to pull her out of the water, or who'd actually done it. She'd assumed it was Acton—since he'd mentioned that Seamus Riordan had shown him where she'd gone under—but it may have been Riordan, himself, who'd dived-in johnny-on-the-spot. It was truly strange that she was unacquainted with the particulars, but she should find out; if it was indeed Riordan who'd come to her rescue, she'd have to gird her loins and thank him.

The loins-girding would be necessary because Seamus Riordan was someone Doyle wanted to avoid. She'd discovered—on that disaster-day, as a matter of fact—that Riordan was yet another fey Irishman. The young man usually lived in Dublin, but he'd been in town because he was a protected witness for the artwork case, and the circumstances were such that he'd felt it necessary to confide in her—in the same way that she'd once felt it necessary to warn Williams.

But the young man's revelation had opened a massive kettle of snakes for her, since her first instinct was to shun him; she'd never met another like her—at least, not that she was aware—and for whatever reason, it made her very uneasy. And she didn't dare tell Acton, since Acton was always terrified that she'd be shanghaied into the shadowy intel services if anyone exposed her.

Her husband was overreacting, of course; even if someone held a suspicion, they'd dare not voice it aloud because no one would believe it. Mayhap in olden times they would have—and she'd have been burnt at the stake as a result—but nowadays, people were less likely to believe in supernatural powers. Not that she'd supernatural powers, of course; only see how she couldn't guess the Lotto numbers no matter how hard she concentrated.

So; poor Acton was jumping at shadows, and as an example you need look no further than the Santero—a former suspect in a murder case—who was, of all things, a voodoo witch-doctor. The Santero had recognized Doyle for what she was, but he was thought to be madder than a hatter and so no one paid him any mind. And then he'd got himself murdered by a person or persons unknown—which was not much of a surprise, all in all. It would be better to take any other career path, one would think, than to settle upon being an evil witch doctor—very unlikely you'll make old bones.

Mentally she shook herself, since she was going off-topic and the topic was who could get close enough to give Acton a taste of his fist.

Suddenly struck, she wondered for a moment if mayhap she'd got it by the wrong leg—mayhap it was a woman. Wouldn't it be more likely that Acton would take a swing from a woman, than from a man? But even using that assumption, no potential candidate sprang to mind. Callie, Acton's half-sister? The younger girl had a fine temper, but it was hard to imagine Acton's not putting the lass into a head-lock with no further ado. Acton's old girlfriend, Melinda? No, Melinda was still holidaying in Paris, as far as Doyle knew. And anyways, Melinda didn't seem a likely candidate; whilst Acton might allow Melinda to take a swing at him, she was not someone who would care to expend the energy.

Lizzie Williams? No; Lizzie would no more hit Acton than she would fly to the moon; it was that strange lord-of-the-manor mentality that Doyle saw amongst the Trestles-folk—they'd all defend Acton to the last yard.

On the other hand, it wouldn't hurt to try to pump Lizzie for information—she tended to be a keeper-of-secrets, but Doyle knew her vulnerable points and could exploit them. Mayhap she'd do a bit of winkling, when they met for tea today.

Her thoughts were interrupted when Tommy, their youngest, bounded up to ask his daily question about whether he was old enough to go to school with Edward yet.

"Not yet, Tommy," she informed him with a hug. "But it's comin', I promise."

With Reynolds' assistance, she managed to get the boys into their coats and mittens and then called down to Acton, "We're off, Michael; step lively or you'll be left behind."

"Step on ivy," Tommy called out to his father importantly.

"Certainly," said Acton, as he emerged from the stairs and lifted the little boy without breaking stride.

"Your coat, sir," said Reynolds respectfully.

Acton shrugged into his coat as he held Tommy alternatively beneath each arm, the little boy shrieking with laughter at being thus handled. "Thank you, Reynolds."

"Thank you Reynolds!" Tommy shouted.

"Faith, what a din," said Doyle.

"I get to push the button on the lift—it's my turn," Edward informed them as he raced out the door and into the hallway.

"You forget your rucksack," Doyle called out to the boy, as she lifted it from the hall table.

"Have a pleasant morning, madam," Reynolds said as he held the door for them. "Sir."

"Don't get into the lift, Edward; wait for us," Doyle called out as she hurried past.

"Thank you, Reynolds," said Acton politely, and walked past with Tommy giggling uncontrollably under his arm.

CHAPTER 6

Her hair was shining in the sunlight.

They began the excursion to St. Margaret's, Doyle walking alongside her husband whilst he pushed Tommy's push-chair; the toddler was at the stage where he wanted his father to do everything since he was suddenly found to be much more intriguing than the boy's all-too-familiar mother.

Their residence building was across the street from a large park—with St. Margaret's School on the far side of that—and so Doyle liked to start-out their mornings by walking their eldest to school. She was not one for any sort of exercise, but she'd been originally shamed into it because she could only imagine what her mother would have said about having servants walk children to school.

However, she soon discovered—rather to her surprise—that she did enjoy the morning walk; you'd no choice but to have a few minutes of quiet reflection which was much-appreciated. That, and she enjoyed seeing the seasons change in the trees.

In the usual course of things, Acton would had left for work by now—he tended to be an early-riser—but since he was currently in the CID's dog-house he was instead pushing a push-chair and discussing with Edward the kinds of birds that were hopping along in front of them on the pavement. Hard to imagine that the man had ever anticipated that this would be his role, one day, but here he was and in all things give thanks.

"Is that a green finch, da?" Edward asked excitedly, indicating a bird on the pathway up ahead.

"A blue tit, I think," Acton replied.

"Faith, but havin' children cuts down on your ability to make saucy remarks," Doyle mused to no one in particular.

"They didn't seem very blue to me," her husband replied. "Seemed very rosy, instead."

"Mayhap a bit plumper than the usual," she offered.

"Any shape or form is completely acceptable."

She laughed, which seemed to remind her husband to ask, "Shall we have McGonigal come by this afternoon? I think you are due for an OB check."

This was his way of letting her know that he'd already made the arrangements for an appointment; Doyle was a bit gun-shy when it came to doctors of any stripe, and since she'd a bad experience with her former obstetrician Timothy McGonigal had stepped-in to deliver Tommy at home. And as could be expected, Acton was not best-pleased about all this, being as he could pick up a phone and summon the royal physicians, if he chose. He'd humored her, thus far, but she'd known that sooner or later they would be having this very conversation.

Easily, she replied, "Let's push him off, Michael—I'm dyin'

to get out and about this afternoon, and recall that I'm supposed to meet Lizzie Williams and pretend to drink tea."

He glanced at her with a touch of concern. "Are you certain you feel up to it?"

She rested her hand in the crook of his elbow. "I do—and if I feel the slightest hint of brain-damage settin' in, I'll have Trenton bundle me home. Not to worry."

"Very well. I will set-up McGonigal in the next few days, then."

"Tell him we're plannin' on another home birth, while you're at it."

There was a small pause. "Very well."

Well, that was easy, she thought in surprise. Of course, he'd mentioned that he wasn't best-pleased with her medical care at the hospital, so that might explain it. She squeezed his arm in gratitude. "All will be well, my friend; I come from hardy peasant-stock, and it's not as though I haven't done it before, easy as eggs."

"With excellent results," he agreed, and leaned to kiss her.

"A magpie!" Edward shouted.

"A blackpie!" Tommy copied his brother as best he could.

"Excellent," said their father.

Edward ran ahead—on the prowl for more birds—and Doyle asked, "Do we know when Miss Cherry's tyin' the knot?" Their current nanny—who was much-loved—was to be married soon; she'd met a retired Irish policeman when the family was holidaying in Dublin and the two had hit it off.

"The month after next, I believe."

"We'll need to hire another nanny." This, spoken with a full measure of dread in that the House of Acton hadn't much luck when it came to nannies, being as the bad ones tended to be back-stabbers of the first order and the good ones tended to be snatched-up into marriage. "We could always have Callie help out until we can find someone who's not tempted to steal the silver."

"Very true," he said in a neutral tone.

This faint praise was to be expected; in the recent past, Acton had discovered that he'd a younger half-sister—being as the previous Lord Acton had been an all-around horror-show, and had forced himself upon Acton's youthful girlfriend. This revelation hadn't made for a smooth road, however, in that Callie tended to be a bit hot-headed and Acton wasn't the sort to abide hotheads—save he'd no choice with Callie, because she was related to him and his wife was forcing him to.

Doyle offered, "Callie's attitude's much-improved, Michael—and the boyos love her."

"She is attending university," he reminded her.

"I know, but mayhap we could work-out somethin', dependin' on her schedule; I'd love to enlist Callie into the household."

Since Acton wouldn't love it, he made no direct answer but instead remarked, "We could consider Javid, perhaps."

Doyle wasn't certain she'd heard him aright, and blinked. "*Javid?*"

"Javid," he affirmed.

"I imagine she's far too busy, Michael," Doyle ventured. "Not to mention she's a murderess."

He tilted his head. "The circumstances were compelling."

Diplomatically, she nodded, reminding herself that her wedded husband was not one to shrink whenever he thought a spot of murder was called-for. But the suggestion was completely unexpected; Javid was a famous artist—indeed, she'd done both their portraits—but the public was unaware that she'd taken a leaf from Acton's book and had decided—

based on her own terrible, past experiences—that some people were better off dead.

After Doyle decided that she'd rather not enter into yet another murder-is-bad discussion with her husband, she instead noted, "She'll be havin' her own baby soon, Michael."

"Yes, but we could easily accommodate her infant along with our own. It was just a thought."

A very, very odd sort of thought, thought Doyle.

Her husband smiled slightly. "You will be surprised to hear that Sir Vikili has agreed to volunteer for the Indigent Defense Fund."

She turned to gape at him. "Holy Mother—they should build a shrine on the spot, because that's *truly* a miracle."

"He'll start with just a few cases, to test the waters."

Sir Vikili was Javid-the-artist's husband, and rather famous in his own right—or infamous, depending upon how you looked at it. He was the premier criminal defense attorney in London which meant he was first, very wealthy and second, had a lot of very smoky and powerful clients. Sir Vikili and Acton tended to lock horns on a regular basis, being as Acton was the premier detective for the Crown on the same high-profile cases that featured Sir Vikili.

The two men had an interesting relationship in that—despite being on different sides of the war, so to speak—they were courteous and respectful toward each other. Indeed, each had done personal favors for the other, based upon that respect—

Oh, Doyle suddenly realized; that's why my husband floated the Javid-as-nanny idea—it's possible that Javid could wind-up in the dock for murder, and Acton's trying to throw a mantle of protection over her in the event her misdeeds are brought to light. Not that he'd much of a mantle to throw, at present—which reminded her of yet another mystery to be laid atop the black-eye mystery; why had the man been suspended, and why hadn't he used the leverage he always seemed to have over everyone to wiggle out of it?

Made uneasy by these troubling thoughts, Doyle decided to test the waters, a bit. "Mayhap Sir Vikili is tryin' to get a few good-works under his belt in the event the prosecutors go after Javid."

"Quite possible."

She eyed him sidelong. "*Are* the prosecutors going after Javid?"

"I am on leave," he reminded her. "I am out of the loop."

This was a patented Acton non-answer because the man's office in their flat had the capability to monitor anything he wished to monitor, and it had not escaped her attention that, upon their arrival yesterday, he'd gone there almost immediately and spent an hour behind closed doors.

She sighed. "I know you think this particular sleepin' dog should be left to lie, Michael, but I'm of two minds about it."

Indeed, she'd had a similar dilemma on several occasions in the past; someone they knew was guilty of murder, but the circumstances were such that Acton—and Doyle, more reluctantly—had decided that the greater good would be served by sweeping it under the cold-case rug.

It always made her very uneasy, because they were supposed to be police officers and sworn to uphold the law—not to mention that murder was a mortal sin. But amongst the many other things that had changed when she'd married her husband, Doyle had begun to realize that things weren't always as black-or-white as she'd thought they were pre-Acton; instead, justice seemed to be a complex balancing-act, often with the least-worst outcome as the goal.

And the upper levels of law enforcement were forced to

constantly recalibrate that give-and-take, because the best criminals were also very good at not leaving any footprints behind. Therefore—even though she didn't approve of her husband's questionable exploits—she could understand what motivated him; there were times when justice would come at too great a cost, just as there were times when the police were unable to come up with sufficient evidence to prove something that—nonetheless—they knew for certain.

And, as an excellent case-in-point, you need look no further than this artwork-rig. The police had long been aware of the operation but it was very difficult to prove money-laundering outright, since there was always a plausible excuse for misguided patrons to overpay for artwork—no crime in that. But the CID had been tantalizingly close to rolling-up this massive international scheme because they'd managed to come up with a prime witness—Seamus Riordan, the fey Irishman who Doyle didn't want to think about.

Riordan had been working in a library at Trinity College in Dublin, where some of the questionable artwork had been stashed on its money-laundering journey through Europe; it would be bought and sold and re-bought and re-sold at inflated prices so as to obscure the origin of the funds. Indeed, the marina-fire had been set in a desperate attempt to destroy the artwork evidence because the criminals had caught wind that the CID was about to start making arrests.

Reminded, she asked, "What's the status of the artwork case? Is all the evidence in smolderin' ruins?"

"Much of it," he replied.

She glanced over at him. "With the London players dead, I imagine everyone else is runnin' for cover."

"We shall see. The investigation continues."

"Would Riordan still be considered a protected witness?"

"Yes," he affirmed.

Doyle decided to drop the subject, because her husband was being mighty tight-lipped. He didn't like to talk about that disaster-day, and small blame to him since it was a thoroughly forgettable experience—not only was his wife knocked-out, but the long-awaited criminal case had been knocked-out, too.

"A kestrel!" Edward exclaimed.

"A petrol!" Tommy loudly agreed.

CHAPTER 7

Perhaps he'd install a piano on the new floor.

That afternoon, Doyle met Lizzie Williams for lunch at a fancy tea café in the business district—not that Doyle had the remotest interest in drinking tea; instead, she'd chosen the place strictly for its strategic location.

Nowadays, Lizzie Williams was working only part-time at the CID's forensic lab, being as she'd two small boys, herself. But it was to be expected that she'd keep her oar in, because she was one of Acton's absurdly loyal Trestles-people, and due to her position in the lab she was able to manipulate evidence to suit whatever questionable scheme he had in mind.

The eating establishment was a new one, even though it was intended to evoke tea-rooms from a by-gone era, with its many-paned windows and elegant chandeliers. It was busy at this time in the afternoon, mainly because it was featured in all the tourist guide-books and nothing said Old Blighty to tourists like taking a dish of fancy tea in a fancy tea-room—especially when you could buy merchandise to commemorate the occasion.

As could be expected, Lizzie had come early to acquire a prime table and the other young woman rose to greet her. "Hallo, Lady Acton,"—Doyle was always "Lady Acton" to Lizzie, no matter how many times she tried to establish a first-name relationship—"I hope you are fully recovered."

"Right as rain," Doyle replied cheerfully as they sat down. "How are your boyos? Between us, it's a wonder that we've a single nerve left."

Lizzie smiled her grave smile. "Thomas doesn't know how I bear the noise."

Doyle laughed. "I think mothers are hard-wired not to be bothered by it, else we'd just murder them outright—like those jungle-monkeys."

Lizzie regarded her with a full dose of skepticism. "There are monkeys who murder their children?"

"There are," Doyle insisted. "I saw it on the telly, once."

The other woman cautioned, "You can't believe everything you hear, Lady Acton."

"Well, it seemed plausible to me. Monkeys are screechers, after all—you can see the mothers gettin' to a flash-point and doin' 'em in." She considered this, as she opened the menu with little enthusiasm. "We see that sort of thing a lot in our business, actually. One time, a husband killed his wife just because she forgot to buy eggs."

Lizzie said dryly, "Sounds more like mental illness, looking for an excuse."

"Aye," Doyle agreed. "A lot of that, goin' around, too—half the jury's goin' to feel sorry for him, since the poor man just wanted his eggs."

"Thomas talks about that—about how you can't always assume everyone else sees things the same way the police do."

Doyle nodded. "Aye. A jury could very well conclude that the killer had good intentions and feel sorry for him, whereas the prosecutors tend to be a cynical bunch, based on hard experience. On the whole, juries tend to be more merciful, so I suppose it's a good thing that they get the final say."

"I suppose." Lizzie perused her menu-card. "What will you have? Have you decided?"

"Just lemon-water for me."

With some surprise, Lizzie ventured, "They have some decaffeinated brews. And the tea-cakes look delicious."

"No, thanks; I'm havin' far too much butter as it is—not to mention that tea's a sorry excuse for a cup o' coffee. Although I will say I'd no idea there were so many different types."

Lizzie explained, "It's all from the same tea plant, though. The different teas come about depending upon how the plant is processed."

Now it was Doyle's turn to eye her companion with a full measure of skepticism. "But there's black, and there's green. And there's that grey one, too, that everyone seems to like so much."

"All the same plant," Lizzie affirmed.

After deciding that tea didn't deserve arguing about, Doyle cast about for a change in topic. "How's our Thomas?"

"Busy, of course, with Acton on leave. Although he got into a scuffle—I told him he had to be more cautious."

There was a small pause, and then—carefully controlling her reaction—Doyle joked, "Got himself clocked, did he?"

"It wasn't serious; a few cuts and bruises from a take-down."

With a smile, Doyle remarked, "Faith, there's no hope for the man; doesn't he know that the whole point of gettin' into the upper-ranks is that you get to tell someone else to go chase a perp, instead of havin' to do it yourself? What exactly happened, d'you know?"

"He wouldn't give me the details, which is probably just as well; I'd only worry."

This was all very interesting, and Doyle considered the extraordinary possibility that it was Williams, who'd taken a swing at Acton. She then decided it didn't seem likely—Acton wasn't going to go lightly with Williams if Williams went on a rampage.

Besides, Williams was Acton's chief henchman at the CID, and was no doubt Acton's main conduit for information at the present time. Because—for some reason—her husband was carefully monitoring what was being said, over at headquarters. It was always possible that he was merely accessing information about his suspension, but she'd the feeling—based on long experience—that it was nothing so ordinary; the man was unsettled, and waiting for the trumpet to sound.

Aloud, she asked, "Does Thomas still confer with Acton on his cases? Or is he supposed to shun him until his suspension is over?"

Lizzie lifted her brows. "From what I can tell, he checks-in on the regular. Yesterday, as a matter of fact, because Thomas was annoyed that I wandered in with the baby while he was on the call."

This was of interest, and Doyle asked, "What's so secret, I wonder?"

"I didn't hear the particulars—Thomas muted it as soon as he saw me." Her cheeks turning a bit pink, she explained, "I should have knocked first, but I wanted to tell him that I have a backer for the Baby-Mix product."

"Oh—oh, that's wonderful news, Lizzie."

Lizzie had developed an herbal remedy to help alleviate morning sickness—she'd been experimenting with different tinctures whilst she was pregnant, herself—and Doyle knew that the young woman was hoping to sell it commercially. It was a tricky thing, because people were understandably leery about taking anything during the first months of pregnancy, but Lizzie was an excellent scientist and must have convinced someone to take a chance.

Ruthlessly quashing any temptation to dwell on this very interesting subject, Doyle glanced at the time on her mobile and then placed it on the table. "Listen, Lizzie; I'm goin' to dip out the back and head over to the *London World News*—to give them a statement about how I'm doin', and also to give my poor husband a PR boost. Acton wouldn't approve and so you're goin' to have to cover for me, else I'll tell your husband about the time you tried to use witchcraft on him."

"Very well," said Lizzie immediately, since the last needful thing was to have Lizzie's husband made aware that his foolish wife had done such a thing. "What if Trenton comes in and sees that you're gone?"

"Tell him I'm throwin' up in the loo—unmarried men hate to hear about pregnancy troubles."

"Married ones, too," Lizzie observed fairly. "All right."

But as she rose to leave, Doyle wasn't at all concerned; the whole reason she'd enlisted Lizzie in this gambit was because Trenton-the-security-man was the young woman's cousin, and therefore he wouldn't be ultra-vigilant; the last thing he'd expect was that Lizzie would act as an accessory to a Doyle-escape.

Outfoxed our Trenton yet again, thought Doyle with a twinge of satisfaction, as she threaded her way through the tables and toward the back door; a shame that I can't keep score.

CHAPTER 8

After walking two quick blocks, Doyle once again entered the busy offices of the *London World News*, an organization that she'd visited before on several best-be-forgot occasions.

She approached the receptionist and offered in an innocent tone, "I've an appointment with a reporter, but I've left my phone and I can't remember the name."

"The story?" The woman asked with brisk efficiency, pulling up her screen.

"The fire at the marina."

"Got it. It's Rachel Anderson; let me direct you to her office."

"Thanks."

As always, the place was a beehive of activity as Doyle navigated the corridors until she halted before an open office door, and knocked on the door jamb.

The young woman—who was frowning over her keyboard—paused to look up, and then lifted her brows in surprise. "Wow." She was rather plain, a bit plump, and looked as though she hadn't changed her hairstyle since she was a child—which Doyle could relate to, as she hadn't, either.

"Hallo, Ms. Anderson," said Doyle. "May I come in?"

The young woman scrambled to her feet and cleared a stack of papers off a chair. "Of course—have a seat. Are you all right?"

"I am," Doyle replied, and looked forward to the day when everyone would stop asking.

"I'm so glad to hear it. Are you here about Bradford?" This, asked a bit anxiously.

"No, I'm here because I wanted to make a statement, if you're agreeable—to tell the public that I'm fully recovered and to thank them for their good wishes." She paused and then added with a smile, "My poor husband could use a bit of good PR."

The other girl nodded in understanding. "Such a surprise, that he's been suspended. It was all over the news."

"Aye." This was actually something that Doyle had decided to confirm, because she'd been entertaining the rather bizarre notion that Acton hadn't truly been suspended at all—that it was some sort of excuse so as to keep her locked-away at Trestles.

But the woman's reaction confirmed it, and—pretending that she knew more than she did—Doyle vaguely waved her hand. "Well, he had that scuffle, poor man—got a bit banged-up."

Her companion nodded again. "Right—I understand it was quite a brawl."

Doyle paused in surprise, and then—feeling her way—offered in a semi-hearty tone, "Not somethin' you'd expect, certainly."

"No—and I understand the hospital's had to revamp their security; you shouldn't be able to move patients around at will."

Hiding her astonishment only with a mighty effort, Doyle

nodded her agreement. "Aye, that; you'd think that such a thing would be in the protocols, already."

She then fell silent for a moment—trying to decide how to couch another question without revealing her ignorance—when the reporter took the opportunity to say rather anxiously, "I was hoping that you were here with information about the Bradford Song case. Are there any leads?"

Slowly, Doyle shook her head. "I've been on disability leave, and so I haven't been in the loop. Is he a friend of yours?"

"He's one of our Metro reporters—very popular, and has a big following. He disappeared about ten days ago." She paused, and pressed her lips together. "We keep hoping he'll turn up, but it seems less and less likely."

Doyle nodded a bit somberly, since—in this day and age—whenever a city-dweller suddenly sank from sight it was usually not good news. "Do the police have his electronics?"

"Yes; I understand they confiscated everything immediately."

This was also not a good sign, since a missing person's electronics were usually very helpful in determining what had happened. Gently, Doyle suggested, "Have you been checkin' with the morgues?"

"He's not there—or at least, not yet—so I suppose that's a ray of hope."

But Doyle knew that such was not necessarily the case, in that unexplained disappearances often meant underworld activity—murders that would never see the light of day. "Did he cover organized crime? Mayhap he was lookin' under a rock that someone didn't want him to look under."

"No, he tended to cover arts and culture—popular stuff."

"Would you like me to put out a trace?" Doyle offered.

The woman brightened. "If you would, although I imagine

his wife has already done so. It's such a shame; Bradford told me that she was quite ill, and was having a terrible time of it. He was very concerned about her."

Doyle heard a nuance behind the words and decided that perhaps our Ms. Anderson, here, rather envied the man's devotion to his wife. "All right; I'll do it today."

"Thanks—we're all really worried." With an effort, the young woman mustered- up a smile. "Now, what can I do for you? You wanted to make a statement?"

Doyle hedged, "You know—come to think of it—I suppose I should check-in with the Met's PR people before I make a public statement."

"Right," the reporter reluctantly agreed. "Instead, may I say that a source tells me you are fully recovered, and that you wish to thank everyone for their warm wishes?"

Doyle smiled. "That you may."

CHAPTER 9

*T*houghtfully, Doyle made her way back into the café and was somewhat relieved to see that Lizzie remained at the table alone, sipping her tea. It was interesting that Acton had indeed been suspended—although he wasn't lying when he'd told her this, so she wasn't sure why she'd entertained such a bizarre notion—and it was also interesting that it had made the news; you'd think—him being who he was—that they'd try to keep it all a bit more in-house. But the most interesting thing of all was that—apparently—there'd been a donnybrook at the hospital on account of patients being moved about whilst the fair Doyle was herself a patient there. It was all very mysterious.

Lizzie looked up as Doyle sat down again. "Did you accomplish what you wanted?"

"Sort of," Doyle hedged, and tried to decide if she should ask Lizzie outright what she knew about the aforesaid donnybrook. Because mayhap she knew about it and mayhap she didn't, but in either event Lizzie would squeak to Acton quick-as-a-cat, and

Doyle didn't want her husband to know, as yet, that the wife of his bosom was starting to put some puzzle-pieces together.

Therefore, Doyle took a leaf out of Acton's book and deftly changed the subject. "The reporter seemed very interested in the Bradford Song case."

Lizzie nodded as she sipped her tea. "Yes—that's Thomas's case."

"Is it? What's happened?"

"He's a well-known journalist—covers art and culture for the city—but he's disappeared, and the CID thinks it might be foul play. His electronics show that he was going to meet someone at a park in Hampstead, but he was careful not to include any identifying information."

"Drug deal gone wrong?" Doyle guessed. "Or he was gettin' into somethin' he shouldn't, and it was a preemption-murder. What does Thomas think?"

"From what he's mentioned, there are a lot of possibilities. Even though Song's married—and married to a gold-level Police Society benefactress, I might add—he's something of a playboy and has caused a few divorces, among the society set. He also wasn't very ethical in how he gathered information—there have been some privacy lawsuits that the *World News* had to settle out of court."

"Sounds like his was a preemption-murder," Doyle decided. "He's diggin' where he shouldn't be."

"Or he could have been killed by an unhappy husband."

This was a valid point, but Doyle decided, "I think the fact that he was a reporter with a history of stirrin' things up points to a professional hit. Especially if we've no evidence and no leads—unlikely it's an amateur murderer."

With an air of disapproval, Lizzie set down her cup. "It

shouldn't be so dangerous to be a journalist. The world needs them."

But Doyle countered, "Aye; sometimes they're the heroes, exposin' evil, but sometimes they wander into evil themselves—usin' their influence to try to pull the wool."

She then paused, much struck, because the ghost who was currently haunting the fair Doyle's dreams was the pattern-card for this latter type. Maguire had used his influence to stir-up public sympathy for murderers, with the result that they'd gone free to murder again. Of course, he'd later repented of his reporting-sins and had become a vigilante—murdering the very people he'd formerly championed.

So; it was all very ironic, that this Song fellow tended to misuse his power and then had disappeared whilst arranging to meet a witness in a park—that was exactly how Maguire had murdered his victims. Maguire, who—coincidentally—was haunting Doyle's dreams.

Doyle's scalp prickled, and she raised her gaze to the tea room's paned windows. Acton famously didn't believe in coincidences, and Doyle had to concede that the man was usually shown to be right. But surely, this reporter's disappearance had nothing to do with Maguire's park-murders, back in the day? After all, the ghost himself had said he was trying to do a favor for a friend—it didn't sound as though it had anything to do with his past misdeeds. Instead, he was urging her to find out what had happened after the marina-fire—that was why he'd sent her to the newsroom, in the first place. It seemed very unlikely that Song's disappearance was in any way connected.

Nevertheless, she felt compelled to ask, "When, exactly, did Song disappear? I told the reporter I'd put out a trace, but I take it that the case is well down the road from that."

"Last known sighting was ten days ago. I think they're investigating, still."

Doyle nodded, since this meant the reporter's disappearance didn't coincide with her hospital stay—which was now going on two weeks ago. Instead, he'd gone missing after she'd already been bundled off to Trestles—no apparent connection, then. "No leads?"

"Thomas hasn't said."

Food for thought, Doyle decided, but I can't let myself get distracted; I've got to unweave the tangled threads that my wedded husband is weaving; threads that apparently include—of all things—a donnybrook at the hospital. She then glanced at the time. "I should head back; thanks for coverin' for me."

"My pleasure," Lizzie said dryly, since she hadn't been given much choice in the matter.

CHAPTER 10

*He wondered if he would ever be easy about her.
Not that it mattered.*

Upon her return to the flat, Doyle sank down on the sofa beside her husband, who immediately brought his hand down the back of her head—he tended to stroke her head when he was worried about her, and she didn't think he even realized that he did it. There'd been more than a bit of head-stroking these past two weeks, poor man—in between those times he was playing unhappy-music at the piano. And meanwhile, he was working very hard to keep a number of things secret from his wedded wife.

"How went your outing?"

"My outin' went excellent—I got to hear all about Lizzie's Baby-Mix. Apparently, she's got a backer."

"Yes. I have lined up an investor—Rolph Denisovich."

Doyle turned her head to stare at him in abject surprise.

"*Rolph* is backin' Lizzie? Mother a' Mercy, Michael; first he's gettin' a medal, and now he's doin' good-works—I've never seen such a turnaround in my life. He's like Zacchaeus in the sycamore tree."

Acton smiled, as the hand resting on the sofa's back idly played with her hair. "We can hope he will put his new fortune to better use than its previous owner."

The reference was to Igor Denisovich, and since the very reason Rolph's uncle was now dead sat beside her, Doyle viewed him with a suspicious brow. "What on earth are you up to, husband?"

Thoughtfully, Acton raised his gaze out the windows for a moment. "Some guidance is needed, I believe. Rolph is ill-equipped to handle such a large sum of money."

Suddenly struck with an ominous thought, she warned, "Don't you dare take over Igor Denisovich's rigs, Michael—I won't stand for it."

Since the dead uncle had been a notorious Russian mafia kingpin, this was not beyond the realm of possibility; in the past, Acton had shown that he was not above taking over a criminal enterprise so as to enrich the coffers of the House of Acton.

"Of course not," he soothed, and pulled her against him. "But Rolph may not have the best judgment, and I do not mind lending a hand."

As Doyle rested her head against his chest, her brow lightened. "Oh. He saved me from the fire, and so now you consider it a debt-of-honor."

His chest rose and fell beneath her cheek. "I suppose you'd say. I am definitely beholden to him."

Doyle couldn't help but smile at this absurdity. "Who would have ever thought you'd be mentorin' the likes of Rolph Denisovich, Michael? Faith, but you are a strange and wonderful man."

He dropped a kiss on her temple. "Mainly, I hope to steer him away from any others who might seek to take advantage."

This was understandable. "Aye; since there's a fortune at stake, the other villains will be lickin' their chops—mainly because our Rolph is somethin' of a nodcock. Although he's married Tanya, so hopefully she'll settle him down a bit."

Rolph had met Tanya, an unemployed housekeeper, during their perilous adventure at the marina and—in the time-honored manner of persons who share perilous adventures—the two had fallen instantly in love.

"I am meeting with him very soon as a matter of fact, and I should prepare. If you will excuse me? And perhaps you should rest for the remainder of the afternoon, Kathleen; I will ask Trenton to fetch Edward from school."

"Aye, then," she agreed. She wasn't tired, but it would be no hardship to spend a quiet hour thinking over what needed to be done, and how to best accomplish whatever-the-plan-was-going-to-be without upsetting her unsettled husband. Because—make no mistake—he was unsettled; on edge, and waiting for whatever-it-was he was waiting for. Which only confirmed Maguire's hint about trap-setting; apparently her husband had a weighty plan unfolding—even though it seemed unlikely, with his being thoroughly sidelined and having nothing better to do than walk little children to and from school.

With a knit brow, she considered this strange concurrence of events. She'd been injured in the past by evildoers, and in the usual course of things her husband would be focused like a laser-beam on five-alarm vengeance; not only would he want to smite his enemies out of sheer bloody-mindedness but he'd also want to make it clear that anyone who threatened his family would be shown a swift and terrible fate. But in this instance, something else was cooking—he'd spent all those hours at the piano, after all. She'd the sure sense he was waiting—waiting and listening. For what, though?

He wasn't after Rolph—she knew this as a certainty, despite the unexpected development that her husband was taking a keen interest in Rolph Denisovich's new fortune. Instead, Rolph would be protected his whole life long because he'd helped save the fair Doyle. Same as with Thomas Williams and Philippe Savoie, who'd each saved her life, once upon a time; Acton owed them a debt-of-honor and Acton honored his debts—it was all very old-world. Faith, if there was any method to her husband's madness it was this; he honored his debts, when it came to his wife.

Her scalped prickled and she wasn't a'tall surprised that it would, since she was well-aware there was something here that she hadn't yet grasped. Something having to do with the missing reporter, and the donnybrook at the hospital, and her husband's being honor-bound.

I need to set-up another lunch, she decided with a sense of resignation; not that I'm a lunching sort of person, but needs must, when the devil drives. Therefore, she pulled her mobile and rang-up Detective Inspector Isabel Munoz.

"Doyle. How are you?"

The fact that the other detective had even asked was an indication of her concern—and since this was about as concerned as Munoz tended to get, Doyle assured her, "I'm right as rain. Let's meet for lunch, I'm bored to flinders."

"Nothing too long." Munoz may be semi-concerned but she'd a full docket and was not one for lunching, either.

"I'll make it easy—we'll just go over to the Deli. Enlist Williams, if you would."

Doubtfully, the other girl cautioned, "He's really busy."

"So are you, but I'm married to the C.O. for the both of you."

"Good point. All right. Tomorrow before noon, so we beat the rush."

"See you then."

Reynolds had been clearly eavesdropping, and he now ventured, "Another lunch, madam?"

In a casual tone she replied, "I miss my friends from work, Reynolds, and I hate bein' out of the loop. I'm not cut out to be idle-rich."

"Perhaps you might consider pacing yourself, madam."

Since it was obvious Acton had given the servant strict instructions to keep his mistress tightly constrained, she assured him, "I'll tell Acton about it—not to worry. But I'll go mad if I let the man wrap me up in cotton-wool, Reynolds, and there's more than enough madness goin' around already."

There was a small pause, and then diplomatically the butler offered, "I might venture to say that Lord Acton wishes only the best for you, madam."

"Aye—I'll grant you that. But the stickin'-point is that my husband's definition of 'best' doesn't always match my own, my friend. And speakin' of madness, did you hear that he's havin' Rolph come over for financial advice?"

"Yes, madam. A very surprising turn of events."

Doyle informed him, "Rolph's going to bankroll our Lizzie, of all things. She's come up with some sort of supplement that eases mornin' sickness for pregnant women; faith, if it works, she'll be crowned Queen of the World—or Queen of the Mums, anyway, which would count as the same thing."

The butler raised his brows. "Is that so, madam?"

"Aye—she's put some herbs together, and even Munoz admitted that it seemed to work. Amazin', that mothers put up with so much and are happy to do it—although there's those monkeys who up and kill their children when they've had it up to here."

The servant offered, "I believe you refer to tamarins, madam."

Doyle brightened. "Aye; that was it—tamarins. Fancy that, I knew somethin' Lizzie didn't, even though she's so crackin' smart."

"If I may say so, madam, you have your own brand of wisdom."

Doyle laughed. "No—now you're doin' it too brown, Reynolds. If I were half as smart as everyone else, I'd have figured out why I wound-up under lock-and-key at Trestles instead of here at home." She eyed him.

There was a small pause. "Perhaps Lord Acton thought you would be more comfortable at Trestles, madam."

"Fah—I don't think anyone's ever been 'comfortable' at Trestles, Reynolds. And it seems very odd that he pulled me away from the hospital whilst I was still knocked-out."

Carefully, the butler suggested, "I believe Lord Acton decided that the hospital wasn't an optimal environment for your recovery."

She made a wry mouth. "Sounds more as though he flounced-off in a huff, for some reason. I hope it wasn't you who gave him his black eye."

This, of course, was the rankest heresy and the butler replied rather stiffly, "Not at all, madam."

She eyed him again. "Then who did, d'you know?"

"I do not, madam."

This was true, but again she'd the impression that the servant knew more than he was saying. Best not tease the man any further, though—it seemed clear he wasn't going to tell her any more than Acton would allow him to. Turning away, she sighed, "Mother a' Mercy, it seems that there was a lot goin' on. whilst I was out-for-the-count."

In a wooden tone, Reynolds asked, "May I bring a pillow, madam?"

CHAPTER 11

In due course, Reynolds opened the door to Rolph Denisovich, the rather feckless young man who'd nonetheless displayed unexpected heroism during the marina-fire. Accompanying him was his new bride, the former Tanya Senak, and the two were radiating sheer happiness.

I never got to experience that newlywed feeling, Doyle acknowledged with a touch of envy, as they all greeted one another. Mainly because I was equal parts astonished and terrified by my own marriage. No matter; it's all turned out rather well—save for the occasional hair-raising adventure. I was never a very brave person, but once I married this husband of mine, I've had little choice but to be brave—and on a regular basis.

With a fond gesture, Rolph squeezed his new bride against his side. "Tanya wanted to come along to say hallo since you were our matchmaker, so to speak."

Doyle smiled warmly, "Hallo, Tanya—and congratulations to the both of you. I'm sorry I missed your weddin'."

"That's all right; it was short and sweet, wasn't it, darling?

Seemed only fitting, given the circumstances." The young man beamed at the memory—even though the aforementioned circumstances included his uncle's death and his hostess's near-death.

For her part, Tanya was wearing a bit too much jewelry for a daytime visit, which Doyle couldn't help but notice even though she wasn't one for knowing the rules for such things. Small blame to the new bride, though; it must all seem like a fairy-tale, where one moment she was unemployed and struggling and the next she's got a doting husband and piles of pretty jewels.

"So, where are the two of you livin'?" They'd plenty of choices, since the late Igor Denisovich had amassed a fortune by purchasing upscale properties in the London area.

"The Haye-Park building," Rolph disclosed with another burst of pride. "Nothing but the best for my Tanya."

Doyle offered, "I know that one; that's where Callie lives—Acton's sister."

"Yes, Lord Acton is the one who recommended it to us."

Now, isn't that interesting? thought Doyle, but before she could contemplate this bit of news, Tanya knit her forehead. "I wanted to ask, Lady Acton—did the police ever find out who killed Mrs. Waring?"

Doyle had first met Tanya when the young woman had been a witness to a case that everyone assumed was a suicide—the wealthy Mrs. Waring, well-known in theatre circles. But—mainly due to Tanya's loyal persistence—a homicide case had been opened, but then had gone cold due to the lack of leads.

Doyle knew very well who'd killed Tanya's former employer, but unfortunately it was one of those greater-good cases that Acton had decided should never be resolved. Therefore, she could only reply with some sympathy, "The CID hasn't much to go on, I'm afraid. They'll keep lookin', of course—hopin' for a lead."

The aforesaid murderess was actually Javid, the portrait artist who was married to Sir Vikili. Javid had apparently decided she'd had-it-up-to-here with her husband's representation of evil people—mainly because she'd been a victim of such, once upon a time—and so she'd committed a few murders of her own so as to send her husband a determined message.

And due to the various interests involved—but mainly because they'd no evidence to convict the artist, in the first place—Acton had determined that the cases should remain unsolved.

Doyle decided she should probably turn the conversation away from dubious people who'd been mysteriously murdered, with Rolph's uncle first in mind. Therefore, she offered, "Your necklace is beautiful." Around her neck, Tanya wore a collection of large colorful gems, each displaying a carved figure.

With a happy smile, Tanya fingered the jewelry. "My wedding present from Rolph. I was so sad, that I lost my pearls in the river."

"Oh; that's a shame—you were that fond of them." Tanya was another person who'd wound-up in the Thames on that disaster-day, and her long string of pearls had been a gift from her former mistress.

Rolph made a sound of regret. "Sent a diver down to look for them, but no luck."

Since this seemed a perfect opportunity, Doyle decided to venture in a casual tone, "I have to say that I don't remember much, after fallin' into the river. 'Tis lucky, we are, that no one was hurt."

"Except for you," Tanya replied with all sympathy. "It was very upsetting, when they could not find you in the water."

"And Tanya insisted that we go to the hospital, to make sure you were all right," Rolph disclosed, very proud of this show of loyalty by his sweetheart.

Her brow troubled, Tanya nodded. "Yes, but—"

"May I offer tea?" Reynolds interrupted. "And here is Lord Acton."

"Good afternoon, Mr. Denisovich, Mrs. Denisovich," Acton said politely, as he approached to shake their hands. "If you would be so good as to follow me to my office?"

"Sure thing," Rolph exclaimed with enthusiasm. "I really appreciate the advice—hadn't thought about half the things you told me. Had a fellow contact me about silver mines in Sheffield—just like you warned would happen. Sent him away with a flea in his ear."

With a polite gesture, Acton included Tanya. "Mrs. Denisovich might also benefit from the discussion. Reynolds, if you would bring the tea-tray downstairs?"

"Certainly, sir."

"This is a great place," Rolph could be overheard saying, as they descended the stairs. "How much did it cost?"

Well, that's of interest, thought Doyle as she watched them leave. Neither my husband nor Reynolds wants me chit-chatting with our Tanya, here, about the incident in question.

CHAPTER 12

He gave Williams a word of warning. Not that it was necessary.

The following day, Trenton drove Doyle over to the Deli to meet her fellow detectives for lunch. The Deli was exactly that—a crowded, slightly shabby establishment within walking distance from Scotland Yard, and therefore often patronized by the personnel who worked there.

Williams and Munoz had arrived before her, and as they greeted one another Doyle duly noted that Williams had an almost-healed cut over his eyebrow. She'd have to be careful about how she approached the subject, however; oftentimes Williams had divided loyalties—what with Doyle trying to minimize all potential law-breaking, and Williams all-in on whatever scheme Acton had going forward. Therefore, their friendship was something of a balancing-act for him—particularly because he was married to Lizzie, who was Acton's loyal vassal in the best medieval tradition.

Detective Isabel Munoz had long been Doyle's rival when it

came to climbing the ladder at the CID, but in recent years their relationship had mellowed somewhat, being as they now had more in common than not; Munoz was married to a fellow-detective and was expecting their first child, a girl who was due in a few weeks.

As they walked over to order at the counter, Doyle jokingly referred to Williams' injury. "Look at you, all battle-scarred; Lizzie told me that a perp roughed you up."

"She's right," he said easily. "Caught me off-guard."

"Best stay sharp," she teased, but privately she was a bit surprised; his words about fighting a perp were true, which meant that she'd been barking up the wrong tree in suspicioning that he'd been hurt in the mysterious hospital donnybrook.

They secured their food, and after they'd sat down at a table, Munoz asked Williams, "Have they made a decision about the Torrance case?"

Williams shrugged slightly as he bit into his sandwich. "I think the prosecutors will press charges."

The other girl grimaced. "Better warn the PR department."

"What's this?" asked Doyle.

Munoz explained, "A mercy-killing case. The press has got hold of it—unfortunately—and they've been shilling hard for a no-charge. Elderly husband killed his wife; she'd dementia and he didn't want to put her in a home."

Doyle grimaced in turn. "Faith, that's a rough one. And since he clearly intended to kill her, you can't just bring a lesser charge—you're stuck with murder-one."

Williams nodded. "It's always a fine line, but that's why we have juries."

This was very true, and another feature of the criminal justice system; even if every element of a crime had been clearly proven, a jury would oftentimes render its own justice—separate and apart from any paltry considerations such as the rule of law. But jury nullification was itself controversial—especially when it came to homicides.

"They might let him off," Doyle agreed.

But Munoz—who like Doyle, was staunchly RC—wasn't having it. "You shouldn't be allowed to kill people just because they're inconvenient. That's not your call."

In a dry tone, Williams noted, "If everyone followed that advice, we'd lose half our caseload."

"But the world would be a better place," Doyle reminded him. "And we could always open-up a shop and sell knick-knacks, or somethin'."

"The Torrance case isn't all that it seems, though," Williams disclosed. "They'd only been married two years, and the dead wife had a tidy little fortune. One of the wife's relatives claims she was already showing signs of dementia when she married the suspect."

There was a small, silent pause whilst the other detectives considered this, and then Doyle offered, "Faith, that does sound a bit fishy."

But Munoz pointed out, "Unless the reporting relative was hoping to inherit, and is now trying to stir-up trouble for the new husband."

"Aye—it's a crackin' tangle-patch," Doyle agreed. "I think you've the right of it; best bring the charge and let a jury sort it out."

Williams nodded. "But in the meantime, the news media is outraged that the husband might wind up in the dock and is doing its best to taint any potential jury."

"A lot of godless people, in the news media," Doyle joked, seizing upon this opportunity to open one of the subjects she wished to broach. "And speakin' of which, Lizzie said you're handlin' the Bradford Song case."

"Yes—and ironically, his was the main voice calling for leniency in the Torrance case."

Doyle raised her brows. "Wow. There's a coincidence—and now Song's disappeared. Mayhap Munoz is right, and the other heirs are on the warpath."

But Williams shook his head. "The two cases don't appear to have any overlap."

Munoz added, "It's not even clear that Song's case is a homicide in the first place; there's no body, and he's the type of man who might choose to disappear rather than face the music—he's got a few skeletons in his closet."

Doyle nodded. "I hear he left some angry husbands in his wake."

"Not just angry husbands. He also used his position at the paper to threaten people—although no one wants to go on record about it. So, it might be that he's disappeared because he went after the wrong target."

Thinking of Kevin Maguire, Doyle could only agree. "Aye—the power these reporters have sometimes goes to their heads. I told Lizzie that his might be a preemption-murder—he got too cocky with the wrong people, and thought he was bulletproof."

But Williams tilted his head in mild disagreement. "Song wasn't an investigative reporter, though; his beat was more along the lines of arts and culture."

"An artist took him out," Munoz joked, being as she was an artist, herself. "I can sympathize—media critics are the worst."

Suddenly struck, Doyle said, "It could be that he stumbled onto some information about the artwork-rig. The perps involved in that one would have murdered him without a second thought."

Williams reminded her, "There's no reason he would be looking into it, though. He wasn't an investigative reporter, remember—he was covering art-shows and galas."

Since this allowed for an opportunity to pursue yet another topic, Doyle asked, "What's the status of the artwork case, anyway? Is it goin' forward, despite the fire?"

"I think everything's on hold, right now."

This was understandable, and Doyle nodded. "I suppose it stands to reason; Denisovich and Elliott are both dead, and you can't have a trial without a defendant."

Munoz offered, "Magistrate Kirken would be a defendant, but he hasn't been arrested yet."

"Oh—oh, that's right," Doyle exclaimed. "Faith, I forgot all about him—he'd be a co-conspirator at the very least." Kirken had been exposed as the corrupt judicial officer who'd been aiding and abetting the marina operation.

Munoz explained, "He was suspended without pay, pending the investigation, but he's decided he's not sticking around and has gone to ground."

This was of interest, and Doyle raised her brows. "Wow—is that so? Have they put out an All Ports Warnin'?"

Williams shook his head. "Remember that he's not been charged with anything, as yet."

"The man's as crooked as a dog's hind leg," Doyle pronounced with a full measure of disgust. "And now he's done a bunk so as to put a pin in it."

Williams conceded, "His flight certainly doesn't help his cause."

"It was a big mistake, not to hold him in Detention," Munoz remarked. "Especially since he's got cohorts who sail across the channel on a regular basis."

Reasonably, Williams pointed out, "They're not going to put

a magistrate in Detention before charges are brought, Munoz. They're just not going to do it—short of a public murder, maybe."

So, Doyle thought; this is all very interesting, and here's a loose-end I forgot about from that whole horror-show. I wonder if Acton is behind the magistrate's disappearance, in the same way that Denisovich and Elliott met sudden and emphatic deaths. I doubt it, since it seems my wedded husband is not hiding his extreme displeasure with the people who were involved.

It's miles more likely that the magistrate saw what had happened to the other two, and decided he wasn't going to hang about to meet a similar fate. He's whistling in the wind, though; his days are numbered. Even if the CID can't manage to track him down, my vengeance-minded husband will—sooner or later. Acton can go scorched-earth with the best of them, but if the situation calls for it, he can be very, very patient. Mainly because he's the grand master at covering his tracks.

Her scalp prickled and she frowned, wondering why it would. It was almost a foregone conclusion that Acton had wreaked a terrible revenge on the two men most responsible for her ordeal—and it also went without saying that he'd done it in a way that covered-up his own culpability. Not a news flash— the man was the next thing to a magician, in getting things to fall the way he wanted. And there was an added benefit, in that all the other players would be made very nervous by these deaths—wondering if they were preemption-murders, and whether they were next-in-line. No one knew how to stir-up a panic better than Acton, after all.

So, none of this was unexpected; her husband was wreaking a vengeance, and no amount of persuasion or appeals to his better angel were going to counter his fury at having to fish his wife out of the Thames. Doyle could call for mercy 'til the cows came home, and it wouldn't matter a'tall—Acton was swinging his sword and Katy bar the door.

The most Doyle could hope for would be to curtail the wreckage and pray that her wedded husband wasn't the one who wound-up in the dock. Although—come to think of it—he *had* wound-up suspended. Faith, it was very unlike him to have to bear any sort of punishment for his misdeeds; usually he was far too wily.

And—speaking of being in the dock—she asked, "Is Seamus Riordan's testimony locked down? I suppose if Magistrate Kirken knows it's all on record, then he's got good reason to flee." It went without saying that Riordan's role had been kept carefully under wraps, since the shy librarian would be an obvious target for a preemption-murder.

Williams replied, "I can't say, either way. The prosecutors are holding their cards very close to the vest."

Doyle nodded. "Can't blame them; Riordan's the prime witness, if they manage to get the case back on track. Although it's a faint hope, to try to keep it a secret—Kirken's a judicial officer, so he's been able to access all the information."

"That does make it tricky," Munoz agreed. "Kirken's not your ordinary suspect."

They sat in silence for a moment, thinking about this, and then Doyle asked, "Is Riordan still in London, or has Acton sent him back to Dublin whilst everything's on hold?"

Williams shrugged a shoulder. "I think his whereabouts have been kept very quiet."

This was true—and somewhat surprising, since Williams was usually up-to-speed on such things. Strange, that Acton hadn't mentioned Riordan in these past ten days—especially since it seemed that the young man had been just as instrumental as Rolph in rescuing the fair Doyle from an early grave.

Williams looked at the time. "I've a meeting—got to go. Good to see you, Kath."

"Be off with you," said Doyle. I'll walk back with Munoz—she's a bit slower, nowadays."

Nettled, Munoz retorted, "I could still take you down, Doyle; two out of three."

"Probably three out of three," Doyle soothed. Let's not put it to the test—you'll jostle the baby."

CHAPTER 13

A shame, that Kirken wouldn't suffer the fate he deserved.

With Williams having left, the two young women began the walk back to the building. "Where's Trenton?" Munoz asked, taking a glance over her shoulder.

"He's somewhere, lurkin' about," Doyle replied easily. "He always is."

"You're not going straight home?"

"No—I'm feelin' fine, and I thought I'd see if you know any good gossip—Williams is too buttoned-up to gossip."

"I don't know a lot of gossip either," Munoz admitted. "With you out, and with Acton on suspension I've been too busy. When are you both coming back?"

"Soon, I think."

"Good. If this baby comes early, our unit is going to be slammed."

"Not your concern," Doyle said with a smile. "You'll be in

your new-baby cocoon, and the outside world will seem a long ways off."

"I'm ready," Munoz admitted. "Geary wants to take some time off, too—depending on whether he's able to." The other woman smiled, as they made their slow progress. "It will be nice, having an excuse to stay home together and do nothing."

Doyle made a face. "Doin' nothin' is overrated, believe me. How's the paintin' goin'?"

"I haven't had much time, being so busy at work. And by the way, I was called on the carpet by Professional Standards about the Maggie O'Day problem, which can be laid at your door. I don't appreciate that at all."

At sea, Doyle raised her brows. "Not a clue, Munoz."

This gave Munoz pause. "Oh—if you don't know about it, maybe I shouldn't have said."

"You've no choice, now. Spill."

"Remember the sketch-artist you brought back from Dublin?"

"Oh," said Doyle, as the penny dropped. "Right—Maggie O'Day."

"Well, she sort of glommed-on to me, and asked if I could help get her paintings some exposure. So, I let her put them up on my website—but then I had to cut ties, because she's been fired from the Met already."

Doyle stared in surprise. "Faith, that was fast. What's happened?"

"Well, apparently she has a huge crush on your driver—the one that's going to university, now."

"She does," Doyle agreed. "Seemed very smitten with Adrian from the first moment she met him."

"Well, she was caught trying to get into the general database to find out more information about him."

"Holy Mother," Doyle exclaimed in dismay. "She sounds a bit nicked."

But Munoz shrugged slightly. "She didn't seem crazy—I didn't have the impression that she was a Section Seven, or anything; I think she's just young and stupid. But it was a dumb thing to do and the fast-track to getting yourself fired." The other girl glanced at Doyle. "Acton hasn't said?"

Doyle blew out a breath. "No, the man's keepin' me wrapped-up in cotton-wool and I'm sick to the back teeth of it. Which reminds me, I want to ask a favor."

"What sort of favor?" Munoz asked suspiciously.

"I want to take some flowers over to the hospital to thank my nurses, but I don't want Acton to know that I'm doin' it, because he'll be all overcome with remorse and such."

"Husbands," Munoz pronounced in an understanding tone.

"So, I'd like to give you my mobile and just don't answer it if it rings—I doubt it will."

Munoz raised her brows, drawing the obvious conclusion. "Acton traces you with your phone?"

"Aye—recall that he's all overcome with remorse and such. Plus, he's worried that my brains have been addled."

"Doesn't seem that way to me," her companion offered with a frowning glance. "Or at least, nothing obvious—you've always been a little scattered."

"Thanks for the vote of confidence. Would it be all right?"

Munoz eyed her. "What about Trenton?"

"I can ditch him," Doyle said with all confidence. "Not to worry."

CHAPTER 14

She wasn't coming straight home, which was worrying.

*A*nd so, Doyle ducked out of headquarters by way of the parking garage, and then caught a cab to the hospital. After purchasing a bouquet in the gift shop, she explained her errand to the security desk who then gave her an escort to the appropriate floor.

Apparently, it's true—that they've stepped-up security, she noted as she followed her escort into the lift. Thanks to the mysterious donnybrook, where patients were moved about and Acton managed to get himself a shiner.

Suddenly struck, she thought—you know, you'd think that Trenton would have been in the thick of whatever-happened but he doesn't seem to bear any battle-scars. Which is more than a bit strange; after all, one would think Trenton's main priority would be to make sure that no one hauls off and hits Acton in the face.

Upon being buzzed-in to the critical care ward, the woman who sat at the desk smiled broadly when she recognized Doyle. "Why, hallo, Lady Acton—how nice to see you."

"I brought flowers," Doyle offered, holding them up. "I wanted to thank you all for takin' such good care of me."

"How lovely; here, let me take them. I'll call-in Isla—she was on your team."

Isla was shown to be a Jamaican woman who immediately glanced toward the hallway. "Did you bring your security-man with you? He's a slice of heaven."

Doyle laughed. "No—Trenton didn't come, I'm afraid."

"Give him my regards," Isla said archly. "And if you have the chance, give him my number."

The desk nurse laughed. "We were saying that it wasn't fair you were surrounded by so many handsome men."

"Tall, dark and handsome," Isla sighed.

"Trenton's blond, though," Doyle teased. "Or are you referrin' to my husband?"

"Well, your husband's a slice too, but so was the other one—you shouldn't keep them all to yourself."

Doyle laughed and thought—a lusty bunch, these nurses; although to be fair, coppers tend to be lusty too—it must come from having to look death in the face on a regular basis.

Recalled to the purpose of her trip, she began, "I wanted to thank you all—apparently it was a bit dicey, what with bein' moved about and everythin'."

The two women stared at her. "What's that?" asked Isla.

Hiding her surprise, Doyle ventured, "I'd the impression that I was moved from one room to the next."

The desk nurse chuckled. "Why would you think that?"

Retrenching quickly, Doyle offered in an embarrassed tone, "Oh—mayhap I was dreamin' or somethin'."

Isla nodded kindly. "That's not surprising—head injuries cause the brain to swell, and the pressure on the brain stem sometimes affects the reticular articulating system."

"Oh," said Doyle.

Patiently, the nurse explained, "It affects your—your overall awareness, I suppose you'd say."

The desk nurse assured her, "Don't worry, you were in an induced-coma protocol and strictly monitored; your husband was all over the doctors and so you were handled very carefully."

"Fancy that," said Doyle, hiding her acute disappointment that there seemed nothing to be gleaned from these two.

"It's a shame Colleen's not here." Isla gave her companion a significant look. "She was your lead nurse."

Seizing upon this faint hope, Doyle ventured, "Is there any chance you could give me Colleen's contact information? I'd love to send her flowers, too."

But Isla lowered her voice to reply, "We're not sure where she's gone. She's done a bunk."

Suddenly on full alert, Doyle managed a casual tone. "Oh? What's happened?"

The woman shrugged. "She didn't show up for work and no one knows where she's gone—she's not answering her phone."

Since the missing woman's fellow nurses didn't seem overly-concerned, Doyle couldn't help but ask, "Aren't you worried?"

The desk nurse shook her head. "Not really; she's been having an affair with a married man and she was saying that she'll be going away with him, soon."

"She's eloped," Isla affirmed, nodding sagely.

"No—she can't elope if he's still married," the desk nurse corrected. "But they went off somewhere together—I think he travels a lot." In a confiding tone, the woman said to Doyle,

"Colleen thinks he's going to leave his wife and marry her. We told her she was living in a fool's paradise, but she won't listen to reason." She rolled her eyes.

But Doyle—who was, after all, a homicide detective—heard a faint alarm go off in her head. "Any chance she's pregnant?" Unfortunately, women who were having affairs with married men and who found themselves in such a state would sometimes also find themselves murdered.

"No—she said she had to be careful not to rock the boat. Was chuffed that she'd bagged her boyfriend—said he'd money, and if it all went as planned, she'd be rich and famous."

"Rich and famous is not all it's cracked up to be," Doyle observed in a doubtful tone.

The desk nurse shrugged. "Couldn't tell her that—she was over the moon, since he was quite the catch. She said he was a news reporter; I don't follow such things, but she said he was famous, and it was one of the reasons she had to lie low—she couldn't be seen with him because it might get into the tabloids."

Doyle stared at her in abject surprise. "Was the reporter's name Bradford Song?"

The nurse hunched her shoulders. "Don't know—she kept it all very hush-hush and frankly, I was sick of hearing about it."

With a mighty effort, Doyle tried to pretend that this wasn't of major interest, and offered-up a bright smile. "Well, please convey my thanks to her, whenever you see her next."

"Will do; glad you're OK."

"And thanks again for takin' care of me—I truly appreciate it."

"All in a day's work," Isla replied easily. With a gleam, she added, "Although your husband was barking orders and keeping us all on our toes. Didn't mind it a bit—he can order me around any day of the week."

"Best stay away from Acton," Doyle warned in a thoughtful tone. "He's a dangerous man."

CHAPTER 15

$\mathcal{U}$tterly perplexed, Doyle stared out the cab window on the ride back to headquarters. What did it all mean? Surely it wasn't a coincidence, that her lead nurse and a reporter were having an affair and now they'd both disappeared? Williams said that Song tended to dabble in what wasn't good for him—he was a bit sketchy. Mayhap it was something, or mayhap it was simply what it appeared to be—love had overcome their good sense, and the two had stolen away—leaving their important jobs behind without so much as a by-your-leave.

Unlikely, she decided immediately. Mayhap my brain's indeed addled, but I think there's something here—even though I haven't the smallest clue what it could be. So, what are the known-knowns? Song has disappeared, and so has his current side-piece, and even their friends at work don't know where they are—although the reporter at the *London World News* is miles more worried than these nurses; mayhap she's got an inkling of what's happened.

And—come to think of it—it's doubly-strange that the nurses

on-site didn't seem to know about the donnybrook at the hospital, but our Ms. Anderson knew. A follow-up visit to the *World News* is needful, I think, to see if I can find out a bit more—after all, Maguire seems to think Ms. Anderson has her finger on the pulse.

Although—although lest we forget, Maguire also said no one knew what had happened save Acton. Which seemed an odd thing to say—surely, *someone* must know *something*?

And then, there was something else—something one of the nurses had said that was significant. Doyle closed her eyes for a brief moment, trying to remember what it was but coming up empty—hopefully it would come to her later. In any event, it seemed clear that some digging into the CID's database was called-for, but—as the poor, smitten sketch-artist found out—the CID kept careful tabs on who signed in, and the fair Doyle was currently off-the-roster. She didn't dare trust Williams with it—Williams was up to his neck in whatever-this-was and had the scars to prove it—and so back to Munoz she must go.

When Doyle returned to headquarters, Munoz was typing at her desk and remarked, "You got a text about twenty minutes ago."

Doyle hurried over to open the text from Acton: "Home soon?"

"Yes," she replied. "Will fetch E from school."

Immediately, another text came—the poor man had been on tenterhooks, waiting to hear from her. "Will meet you there."

Frettin', she thought, as she sheathed her phone; but there's no balm to be had for the man—I'm hot on the trail, even though I haven't the first clue where it leads.

Munoz checked the time. "Got to go; I have a Case Management Meeting."

"Can you give me five minutes, Munoz? One of the nurses

who took care of me is missin' and I'm worried about her. And since I'm on leave, I can't get into the database."

With deft fingers, Munoz pulled it up. "Name."

"Colleen Cadigan."

"More specific—there are a few."

Doyle reminded her, "She'll be printed, since she's a nurse."

"Right. OK, here she is."

The young woman's security badge photograph appeared on the screen—an attractive Caucasian woman who was wearing a bit too much make-up.

"Pretty," Munoz remarked.

"Aye. Can you do a 'whereabouts'?"

Munoz typed in the request and the two detectives leaned-in to scrutinize the results that had appeared on the screen.

Munoz—who could read faster—grimaced. "Oh-oh; no credit cards or calls after the evening of the third."

Doyle found that she was unsurprised and asked, "Can you trace where was she when the lights went out?"

Munoz typed once again, and advised, "Phone was last pinged at a park in Hampstead."

Astonished, Doyle slowly stood upright. "Holy *Mother*, Munoz; I think I know who's killed her. Faith—she must have indeed been pregnant. He's killed her, and now he's lyin' low."

Munoz glanced up in surprise. "Who?"

"Bradford Song—that reporter who's missin'. The nurses told me that Cadigan was having an affair with a reporter—said she was certain the man was going to leave his wife for her—and now she's AWOL."

"Doesn't look good," Munoz agreed in a grim tone.

Thinking about this, Doyle nodded. "Aye, and his wife's a wealthy do-gooder; he'd have plenty of incentive to make certain his latest light o' love didn't rock the boat."

"I should open a file," Munoz decided.

Doyle reminded her, "Williams is already handlin' a 'missing persons' file on Song."

"Oh—right. I'll check with Unit Coordination then—they'll probably give me the lead, since Williams is so busy with Acton's caseload."

The other detective then looked up at Doyle with grudging admiration. "Good catch."

"More like an amazin' coincidence," Doyle demurred, and then was not at all surprised when her scalp started prickling.

CHAPTER 16

Kirken had logged on to the database—good. He'd seen the train ticket.

Doyle had Trenton drive her over to St. Margaret's, where Acton was already waiting by the gate. As he bent to kiss her—a hand cradling the back of her head—she soothed, "I'm sorry, Michael—the time got away from me but I do think I've stumbled across a homicide, for my sins."

Belatedly, she realized that she didn't want to have to confess her unauthorized excursion to the hospital—or her other unauthorized excursion to the *London World News*, speaking of weaving tangled webs—and so she made an attempt to gloss over this unfortunate lapse. "I was talkin' with Munoz, and we think we have a breakthrough on the Bradford Song homicide."

Acton was silent for a moment, and she could sense his profound surprise. "I was not aware the Song case has been designated a homicide."

"Oh—no, it hasn't; instead, I'm talkin' about a homicide that he may have committed. Munoz and I stumbled across somethin' ominous—he'd been havin' an affair with a nurse at the hospital, and the nurse disappeared around the same time he did."

Doyle decided she couldn't mention the lovers' park-meeting without giving the game away, and so she offered, "Song's married to a wealthy society-lady and the girlfriend may have fallen pregnant, which would account for motive."

Acton gazed at the school's ivy-covered walls for a moment. "It seems unlikely that he would decide to disappear, if he indeed killed her."

Doyle had to acknowledge the wisdom of this, and it gave her pause. "Aye; especially someone as savvy as Song—he'd have known that it would only point a bright shiny arrow at him as the prime suspect." She paused, weighing what she should say, and then ventured, "But I don't think many people were aware of the affair, and mayhap he's hopin' no one will connect the dots."

"Possibly," he agreed. "What did Williams think?"

"Williams left before we connected the dots," Doyle hedged. "And anyway, Munoz is goin' to contact Unit Coordination about openin' a homicide file on the nurse, since Williams is already so busy with your caseload."

"A good thought," he agreed, and then their conversation was interrupted when Edward appeared, along with the other children rushing through the gate as though they'd been paroled from a life sentence; their uniforms quite a bit worse for wear than when they'd entered that same gate in the morning.

As they began the walk back home, Doyle listened to her son chatter and duly noted that Acton hung back for a moment to make a call. Her antenna quivered, and she knew—down to the soles of her shoes—that it had something to do with what she'd revealed to him about this Song-Cadigan wrinkle.

Which was another baffling development; Doyle knew—in the way that she knew things—that her husband had not been happy with her report, even though he'd carefully covered-up his reaction. It may only be that he didn't want her doing any detecting, of course, but she'd the feeling it was more than that; he was definitely trying to hide his dismay that she'd turned over this particular stone.

Did he know something unsavory about Nurse Cadigan, mayhap, and was reluctant to allow it to come to light? Certainly, he must have met the woman whilst he was busy making a nuisance of himself at the hospital. Or could the nurse's disappearance be connected to the mysterious donnybrook? That seemed unlikely—after all, there was a ready-made reason for the poor woman to get herself murdered, separate and apart from the goings-on at the House of Acton.

With a mental sigh, she debated whether she should just confess her two secret meetings and take her lumps—he wouldn't browbeat her about it, of course, and a-penny-to-a-pound he'd find out about them anyway—wretched man. Mayhap it would be best to confess—this Song-Cadigan wrinkle seemed important, for some reason, and therefore he'd be bent—as only Acton could be bent—on finding out how his wife had found out what she'd found out. And when he discovered that she'd been sneaking-about and delving into the database, she'd feel guilty because he'd think she didn't trust him, which—when it came down to brass tacks—was exactly the case.

This gave her pause, and she frowned. She didn't trust him—not on this, anyways—because there was something here that he didn't want to tell her—something important. But why was it all so mysterious? Faith, you have a little lapse of consciousness and the next thing you know the world's turned upside-down—

what with the illustrious Chief Inspector suspended, and everyone sporting a six-pack of beat-up.

And strangest of all, no one seems to know what's happened save for Acton—which is exactly what the ghostly Maguire told her. Acton knows what's happened, and he's bound and determined that no one else—including the wife of his bosom—ever finds out. But why? Why was it all such a secret? There was the question that most needed answering.

Deciding that she should make an attempt to knock the man off his pins—mayhap he'd give her a glimpse of what was rattling about in the enormous brain of his—she waited until they came to the playground's gate before saying, "I wish you'd tell me what's got you jumpy as a tick, husband. It can't be good for my recovery to be worried about whatever-it-is that you're up to."

As she'd intended, this gave him pause. Whilst Edward raced over to the playground equipment, he drew her against his side and thought about his answer for a moment. "I did not aquit myself well, when you were injured," he finally said. "And so, I cannot help but feel that the less said, the better."

This was true, and not so very surprising; obviously he'd behaved badly, and even the nurses had hinted that he'd been ragin' about—small wonder that he was ashamed to let her hear the details. He'd been shaken-up, poor man, and he was one who didn't shake-up easily.

With a full measure of sympathy, she brought her other arm 'round his waist and squeezed him fondly, as they walked over to the playground's edge. "No blame to you, Michael—it was a close-run thing. But all's well that ends well; my head is crack-proof, bein' as I come from hardy peasant-stock and we've a long history of bein' conked by our betters."

He leaned to kiss the top of her head. "I am grateful beyond measure. But we must take a step back, perhaps, so as to allow you to fully recover."

She made a wry mouth. "That's a tall order, my friend, when everyone's throwin' homicides across my path. Faith, it's another busman's holiday—the same as when we went to Dublin."

"Nevertheless," he replied, in what was for him a firm tone.

They greeted Miss Cherry, who'd brought Tommy to the playground also—the usual routine, since the two boys needed to expend some afternoon energy or they'd be twin hurricanes by the evening.

Edward proceeded to join his mates in the upper echelons of the jungle-gym whilst Tommy took-up position at the slide, since he'd discovered how to slide down head-first and this was —for the moment—more alluring than copying whatever his older brother was doing.

Acton came to stand beside Doyle for slide-duty, and she decided to ask in a deceptively mild tone, "So; am I allowed to speak about my homicide catch without gettin' shut down, or should I find some other nice man to talk to?"

CHAPTER 17

It was nothing short of extraordinary that she'd found out as much as she had.

As could be expected, Acton was immediately apologetic. "Forgive me, Kathleen. Of course, you may speak of whatever you wish—I am sorry if I was brusque."

With a smile to show that she forgave him, she offered, "You have to admit that it's an interestin' wrinkle."

"It is, indeed."

She paused to duly admire Tommy's technique in sliding down the slide, and then put a hand to the boy's back as he laboriously climbed up the ladder again. "Song would seem the prime suspect for Cadigan's murder—save that he's up and disappeared also, which he'd know was not a smart move. I suppose it's possible that he's not a suspect after all, but instead he's just as dead as she is."

"It is possible," her husband admitted. "Someone of his stature does not simply disappear."

With a knit brow, she reasoned, "Well, if he's not the one who's killed her, that would mean it's about somethin' else, and not about their affair. Williams said Song tended to play a bit fast-and-loose with his reportin'—a brash one, he was, and used his position at the paper to make people knuckle-under."

"I have heard the same."

She glanced at her husband as Tommy carefully positioned himself on his stomach, his little face a study in concentration. "So, mayhap his was a preemption-murder; the wretched man thought he was bullet-proof, but he rattled the wrong cage and found out—the hard way—that he wasn't."

"Certainly, a valid working-theory."

Thinking about this, however, she blew out a breath. "No need to humor me, husband—that's not a decent theory a'tall, because it doesn't explain why Cadigan's dead, too. Unless she was at the wrong place at the wrong time, and found herself murdered when he was murdered."

"Entirely possible."

But Doyle was already frowning as she considered this alternate theory. "Mayhap we're makin' it far more complicated than it needs to be and we're ignoring the most obvious reason of all. Has Williams interviewed Song's wife? Mayhap she's sick to the back teeth of her husband's dippin' his ladle into other cisterns, and so she's up and killed them both."

"I believe the wife has indeed been interviewed." Acton paused for a moment and then added, "She did not report her husband's absence to the police; instead, the initial report was from a co-worker."

Poor Rachel Anderson, thought Doyle; who—like Cadigan, apparently—was a smart woman who was stupidly yearning after the wrong man. Aloud, she offered, "Well, that's of interest—although it may not be as ominous as it seems; the wife may have been reluctant to report him missin', if she was worried that he was dallyin' somewhere—she wouldn't want to shine a light on his doings."

"Entirely possible, given her status."

Doyle made a wry mouth. "Faith, the wretched man may yet show up, which would only serve him right—to see the brouhaha he's caused."

Gently, her husband reminded her, "Not your concern, in any event."

With a sigh, she agreed, "Aye—we're both off the active-roster and shamblin' about on the sidelines. A crackin' shame, is what it is."

"You must rest, Kathleen; I am afraid I must insist."

"I'm not a good rester though, Michael—it's not in my nature." With a sidelong glance, she added, "Neither are you."

But her normally-unrestful husband only answered in a sincere tone, "Perhaps we should take this opportunity, then; we've little choice, after all." He ran a fond hand down the back of her head as they watched Tommy slide down again. "We can relax at home and enjoy the children."

She made a derisive sound. "The Met on its busiest day is more relaxin' than our boyos, my friend. Can't hold a candle."

He smiled. "Nevertheless."

Stubbornly, she insisted, "I think we need to get back in the harness—havin' this case flung across my path is a sign from heaven—like Gideon's fleece." And unspoken was the fact that she needed a plausible reason to go visit the reporter again—very unlikely she could get away with another tea-shop excuse.

"Let's have McGonigal reassess when he comes for your OB check-up. In the meantime, I will ask Williams to open a file on the missing nurse."

Oh-ho, she thought, as she put a hand on Tommy to guide

his ascent up the ladder yet again. He wants Williams to handle this Cadigan matter instead of Munoz, which means it must be indeed connected to the mysterious goings-on at the hospital. How or why, I haven't a clue, but no doubt that's who he was ringing-up, back at the school—Williams, telling him to make certain to snatch this case away from Munoz. Which also means that Thomas Williams knows more than he's saying—not a surprise, since he'd the battle-scars to prove it.

This thought led her to another odd happenstance in what seemed like an unending list of them, and she frowned as she came back around to stand beside her husband. "Why would Williams be handlin' Song's disappearance in the first place? Wouldn't the Missing Persons Unit have jurisdiction?"

But Acton had a ready answer. "Mrs. Song is a high-profile citizen, and so it was thought best that the CID assign a ranking detective to assist Missing Persons."

This seemed reasonable, and she nodded. "Oh—that's right; not to mention that she's a Met supporter—the 'Beneficial Police Society' or somethin'."

"Exactly."

She smiled. "And making-nice to high-profile benefactors—benefactresses?—is usually put on your plate, but since you're currently in the doghouse, Williams is the next man up."

"Something like that."

Mental note, she thought; winkle Williams, to see if he will give me a hint of what's afoot. And truly, I must speak to Ms. Anderson at the *World News* again; I didn't realize, that first time around, that she seems to know more about all this than everyone else put together.

CHAPTER 18

After deciding that she shouldn't dwell overmuch on the Song-Cadigan matter—Acton had a fine-tuned radar when it came to her, and oftentimes he'd know what she was thinking even before she did—Doyle changed the subject. "Speakin' of our Dublin holiday, I hear that the sketch-artist has managed to get herself fired already."

"I have heard the same."

"Faith, you can't go dippin' into the database, no matter how lovelorn you are."

This, said with an air of disapproval and without the slightest hint that Doyle had been doing some unauthorized dipping of her own, just this afternoon. "Has the lass gone back to Dublin to lick her wounds?"

"I imagine." It seemed clear that the poor sketch-artist didn't make the long list of Acton's worries, at present.

Reminded, she asked, "Is Seamus Riordan gone back to Dublin, too? Williams wasn't sure."

"The Met is making arrangements to send him home," Acton said. "We will need to reassess the case, of course."

She nodded, since this aligned with her own conclusion; if the two principals were dead and Kirken was on the lam, there was no one left to prosecute—at least, for the London-based portion of the rig.

Tommy began protesting loudly because he'd sand in his shoes; the toddler hated having sand in his shoes as much as he loved playing at the playground, and so this was a familiar refrain.

Willingly, Acton bent to sit the boy on the slide so as to remove his shoes but Doyle offered with little sympathy, "It's *sand*, Tommy. There's a whole lot of it in the world—you're never goin' to win, and so best just come to terms."

"Da doesn't like sand in his shoes," Tommy protested in the tone of someone who has the winning argument.

"Well, that's nothin' be proud of, my boyo; your da wouldn't last a hot minute workin' in a fish-market, either. You're lucky you've a side to your family that's not afraid to muck-about a bit—this world's a messy one."

"I must protest," Acton said with a smile. "I can muck-about, so long as the muck is fairly clean."

Doyle laughed. "And so long as you didn't get fish-scales caught in the cuffs of your fancy suits."

"Or collect sand in my shoes."

She sighed. "You haven't a clue, my friend—not a lot of sand to be had at a fish-market. But your shoes would come home smellin' something awful, and you wouldn't care for that a'tall; you'd be brusque to beat the band."

"Sadly, I feel that you may have the right of it."

She nodded. "Aye—that's the problem with you aristos; you've never been taught any life-skills, and so all you're good for is smitin' your enemies and guardin' your gold, like the dragon in that famous story."

"The shock of my tail is a thunderbolt."

Doyle laughed. "You're only makin' my point, husband—not sure how helpful it is to pull up quotes at the drop of a hat when you don't know how to debone a codfish."

"Odd fish!" Tommy exclaimed.

"Exactly," Doyle said to the little boy.

Acton stood to draw her to him. "Then I suppose it's a good thing that I am married to one of the plain, quiet folk."

She willingly embraced him back. "You might make light, but it's been your salvation, husband. Mark me."

"As well I know," he agreed, and kissed her.

After the re-fitted boy ran back to the slide's ladder, Doyle decided that—since she'd put her husband in a softer mood—she may as well take advantage. "Did you meet Colleen Cadigan when I was at the hospital? Any insights?" Acton may not have Doyle's perceptive abilities, but he was a very shrewd judge of people in his own right.

"I did meet her," he replied in a neutral tone. "She seemed very capable."

Doyle made a derisive sound at this faint praise. "Oh—not a good impression, then? Well, she may be a capable nurse but she's a bit foolish, if she's havin' an affair with a man that the public knows to be married."

"I cannot disagree."

Warming to this theme, Doyle continued, "Even smart women tend to be dumb when it comes to men. Maggie O'Day is yet another example—it's as though they lose their bearings and forget what's-what."

"Love is a powerful motivator," he agreed. "We see it, often enough."

She hid a smile, thinking this observation very apt, considering how her husband had just carefully shaken every grain of sand from a fussy toddler's socks. "Aye; it's the same old song; people tend to get murdered for love or money—although it's not truly 'love' in that case, because love is supposed to be unselfish and bear-all-things. Instead, it's thwarted-love, and brimful of selfishness."

"A very astute observation."

Suspiciously, she eyed him as she stepped back to watch Tommy. "Are you humorin' me again?"

"I am not, on my honor. Instead, I very much agree with you."

Thinking about this, she added, "Although Williams has got that mercy-killin' case, which I suppose could be the exception—that's sort of an 'unselfish-love' murder. Murder is never the answer, but it makes a compellin' argument—that a husband killed his wife because he didn't want her to suffer any longer."

Acton tilted his head in mild disagreement. "There is a monetary element in that case, though. I will admit that I have yet to come across a mercy-killing that is wholly unselfish."

Since he'd have far more experience in this than she, Doyle raised her brows. "Is that so? But I don't know as it matters, in the end; someone like you or me—knowing what we know—wouldn't see it in the same light as the average person—someone who's mayhap got their own relatives as a case-in-point. It makes you wonder what the jury will do."

"I imagine it will all depend upon the quality of the representation."

"Aye, a skillful barrister can convince a jury of practically anythin'. It's not fair, but there it is. Not to mention that the media's been shillin' hard to let the husband off the hook."

"Bradford Song's was the main voice, as a matter of fact."

She nodded. "Aye—Williams mentioned that. Faith, everythin' seems to keep circlin' back."

"Kathleen—" he cautioned in a gentle warning.

"No need to be brusque, husband. But let's line-up Tim to give me the all-clear, please, so that I'll be ready-to-roll when you're re-activated. When's your hearing, anyway? Hard to believe Professional Standards isn't fast-tracking like mad to get you back in the game."

"Very soon," he assured her.

This seemed to be yet another weasel-answer—not to mention it was very out-of-keeping; her obsessive husband would know down to the minute when his suspension would be over.

Suddenly struck, she realized that she didn't know any of the particulars about his suspension—she'd just assumed it had something to do with the donnybrook and his black eye. But since no one seemed to know about the donnybrook, could it be something else?

Furrowing her brow, she asked, "Exactly why were you suspended, my friend?"

In an even tone, he disclosed, "I was arrested for setting the marina fire."

CHAPTER 19

Doyle gaped at him, thoroughly astonished. "*What?*"

He smiled slightly. "Believe me, my reaction was very similar."

"They *arrested* you?"

"Indeed. Officer Shandera. He was very apologetic."

"Holy *Mother*, Michael." She stared at him in stunned silence for a moment, and then realization hit. "The crooked magistrate," she breathed. "Tryin' to get himself a head start."

He bowed his head. "So, it would seem. Kirken signed the arrest warrant."

"Mother a' Mercy, but there's some brass, for you. Small wonder he's in hidin'."

"I am certain the CID will eventually find him."

She slowly shook her head. "For heaven's sake, Michael; if you were tryin' to murder me, there's no way you'd choose such a clumsy way to go about it—it's like Kirken doesn't know you a'tall. Instead, you'd be smooth-as-silk and have an iron-clad alibi."

He admitted, "The arrest warrant was suspended almost immediately because I did have an iron-clad alibi."

But this was cold comfort to Doyle, who retorted with all frustration, "Still and all, he's got away, the blackleg." She glanced at her husband. "I'd be very much surprised if he wasn't hidin' out overseas, somewhere. Think they'll catch him?"

"I have every confidence," Acton replied. "Kirken is not very steady."

Doyle hadn't met the man, but could only agree. "Aye—it's a clear sign of panic, that he decided the best course was to have you arrested—that's not goin' to fly for a moment with anyone who knows us. And poor Officer Shandera; did he have to haul you into Detention?"

Acton smiled slightly. "No. As a matter of fact, he allowed me to escape so as to attend you at the hospital."

She laughed. "Did he, indeed? Jerry's a good man."

Fondly, she squeezed his waist and thought, God bless Officer Shandera—and now there's another one, who's earned a debt-of-honor from Acton.

Her scalp prickled and she frowned slightly, remembering that it had done so the last time she'd thought about this—about how Williams and Savoie were golden in Acton's book, since they'd once saved the fair Doyle. Acton honored his debts-of-honor—not a news-flash. Why would this cause her antenna to quiver?

"Mum," Tommy complained from his perch atop the slide. "You aren't *watching*."

"I'm watchin'," she affirmed, and duly fixed her gaze on the umpteenth trip down the slide.

After landing at the base, Tommy then decided he'd best check on his older brother which—unfortunately for his parents

—meant that they'd have to go spot him on the more precarious jungle-gym, since Tommy didn't like to be reminded that he wasn't as able as Edward.

As they followed the little boy over, Doyle suddenly realized that something didn't add-up. "If the arrest warrant's been rescinded, then why are you still on administrative leave?"

Philosophically, her husband replied, "Protocol requires that Professional Standards hold a hearing before reinstatement. The process has to proceed."

She eyed him in amusement. "Mother a' Mercy; who are you, and what have you done with my husband?"

But he only reminded her, "I am in no hurry, Kathleen. It is important that we make certain you are fully recovered."

"I'm right as rain," she declared. "Never better."

"We will wait for McGonigal's approval, nevertheless."

Doyle then heard her name called, and willingly abandoned Acton to Tommy-duties as she walked over to greet Mary Savoie and her family, who were also regulars at the playground.

Mary had been Edward's nanny, once upon a time, but now she was happily married to Philippe Savoie—although her route to happiness had been a long and winding one. And it all just went to show that you never knew; Savoie had been a notorious underworld player—a constant stand-out, on Interpol's Watch-List—until he'd fallen hard for the House of Acton's nanny and now he seemed to be—fingers crossed—well on the road to reform. Mary had brought two children into her marriage to the Frenchman and Savoie—who'd never been married—had previously adopted a son, with the result that the blended household was already quite busy as they awaited the birth of another child. Mary's eldest two attended St. Margaret's with Edward, and so they often visited together whilst the children played after school.

Mary was more dressed-up than her usual—wearing a pretty dress, with her hair pinned up—and Doyle offered, "You look very fine, Mary."

"Thank you, Lady Acton—I think this is the only dress that still fits, although it won't for long. We had a meeting with a government grant office this morning."

Doyle heard this news with mixed emotions; the Savoies were managing a bakery with the proceeds going to at-risk youth, and Doyle decided she didn't want to hear the particulars about the meeting, since Savoie had a long and storied history of skimming government money from feckless bureaucrats. Mary might be a good influence on the man, but this particular leopard wouldn't so easily change his spots. Of course, it didn't help matters that Doyle's wedded husband had aided and abetted Savoie in the aforementioned skimming scheme—not to mention that the two men had partnered in other criminal enterprises, along the way. Little did Savoie know, on that long-ago day when he'd saved Doyle's life, that he'd gain a partner-in-crime in the guise of the illustrious Chief Inspector.

Mary, being more naïve than Doyle—which was truly saying something—didn't know any of this, which always left Doyle to carefully guard what she said around the young woman, even though discretion was not her calling. Although it was entirely possible that even if Mary found out about her husband's sordid past it wouldn't matter; Mary was one of those people who saw only the good in everyone, and—as a consequence—she wouldn't last a hot minute in law enforcement.

"How are you feeling, Lady Acton? Or are you tired of being asked?"

"I'm that sick of bein' coddled," Doyle admitted. "Acton

wanted to hole-up at Trestles for a bit longer, but I put paid to the notion—everything's far too quiet, there."

Her scalp started prickling yet again, and Doyle paused in surprise, not really listening to Mary's response. Trestles was always quiet; surely that wasn't anything to kick-up her instinct? Although it did seem as though Acton had trimmed-down the staff quite a bit; she'd assumed that he wanted maximum privacy for her recovery—which only made sense. Acton was a very private person, and it must bother him no end that they were in the thick of a sensational story like the marina-fire. Nonetheless, it was interesting that he'd cleared everyone out; it must have been quite an adjustment for the man, not to have an army of servants at his beck-and-call.

Whilst Doyle was trying to decide why this particular point had caused her perceptive abilities to act-up, Mary leaned down to unbuckle Hannah from her push-chair. As she did so, her coat fell open, leaving Doyle to stare in astonishment at the double length of pearls Mary wore around her neck.

CHAPTER 20

I'm that tired of being gob-smacked, Doyle thought with a full measure of annoyance. But it can't be a coincidence, that the coincidences are pilin' up like a house afire and I'd best get on with whatever-it is that Maguire is prodding me to find out.

Because it wasn't hard to come up with the alarming conclusion that Savoie must have stolen Tanya's necklace—very fond of stealing jewelry, was Philippe Savoie—and he must have lifted it when they were all being rescued out of the river, since that was when it had gone missing. But it was mighty hard to believe that he'd be stealing jewelry whilst his wife and children were being fished out of the Thames—they'd been caught-up in the fire, too.

Her brow cleared. More likely he'd stolen the necklace when they were at the hospital—Tanya had said she and Rolph had gone over to check on the fair-but-unconscious Doyle. But wait —that didn't make sense, either; no one from Savoie's family had been admitted to the hospital, so why would Savoie be there? Of course, Savoie may have wanted to check-in on Doyle, same as Tanya—

Oh, she suddenly realized; I'm forgetting the main thing—I'm forgetting the donnybrook and the mysterious moving of patients. Was Savoie involved? Holy Mother, could it have been *Savoie* who gave Acton his black eye? This was actually plausible, since Savoie was a street-fighter from way back—it was possible that he'd surprised Acton and got in under his guard.

With some confusion, she looked up to observe Savoie, standing at the playground's edge to keep an eye on his two older children and apparently paying no attention to Acton, who was busy trying to keep Tommy from major bodily harm. Were they angry with each other? It was hard for even her to tell, because the two men were past-masters at hiding their emotions. Was Savoie beat-up? He didn't look to be. It was all very strange, but here was the string of pearls, big as life, and there was no time like the present to do a bit of probing.

Mustering up an admiring tone, Doyle ventured, "What lovely pearls, Mary."

With a smile, Mary fingered them as she balanced little Hannah on her hip. "Oh—aren't they? I'm usually not one for jewelry, but Philippe thought I'd like these." She lowered her voice to confide, "Even these are a bit much, but it makes him happy and so I'll wear them whenever I have to dress-up a bit."

"You've a dotin' husband, Mary. Were they for a special occasion?"

"No—he gave them to me after the fire." Mary then added with a full measure of sympathy, "He felt so badly about all of it—felt badly that he was away."

Doyle blinked. "He was out of town?"

"Yes—he'd gone to Bristol, for business. And it was just as well, really—he'd have been so upset."

Doyle could only agree, having seen Savoie furious, and on more than one occasion. Faith, Savoie's fury could rival Acton's fury and at times, it had. But there was obviously more to this story; if Savoie had come pelting back from Bristol, it seemed a little strange that he'd come to visit Doyle at the hospital rather than go check on his own family. Unless he wasn't at Bristol to begin with—there was always that possibility.

"All's well that ends well," said Mary, which was just the sort of thing Mary would say after having experienced a near-death disaster.

For her part, Doyle's thoughtful gaze rested upon the two men. I don't think whatever-this-is has ended—well or otherwise, she decided. Not by a long shot.

Therefore, she excused herself and strolled over to have a little visit with Savoie—it would have to be a short conversation, and so she cut to the nub. "Ho, Philippe; been scrappin' in any donnybrooks, lately?"

Amused, the Frenchman lifted his brows. "Yes? What is this?"

"A fight—a brawl."

With a small smile, Savoie made no response but only tilted his head slightly, which only affirmed Doyle's suspicions.

"You should tell me, my friend. I think it might be important."

With a show of modesty, her companion shrugged his shoulders. "I do what I am told."

"Pull the other one, Philippe; you're the last person to do what you're told."

"*Non, non—c'est vrai*," he insisted. "I am called to be the Saint Bernard, and so I come."

This was true, and it made her reassess her theory, as it seemed that Acton had called-in Savoie for an assist rather than coming to blows with the man—which was a relief, all in all; talk about a clash of the titans, that would take the palm.

"Well, Tanya Denisovich misses her pearls, Philippe. They were important to her."

"Her husband, he can buy her more pearls." This, said with a thread of derision because Savoie wasn't a big fan of Rolph Denisovich, stemming from a certain dinner-party they'd both attended.

"Well, these particular pearls are special—they belonged to a king, or somethin'."

Her companion considered this in silence and Doyle belatedly realized that mayhap this little revelation wasn't exactly helping her cause. "At least, don't let Tanya see them, else she'll put two and two together and figure out that you filched them."

"Mr. Savoie," said Acton, as he approached with a protesting Tommy firmly in hand. "Well met."

Doesn't want me talking with Savoie, either, Doyle concluded. Doesn't want me talking with anyone who knows what happened at the hospital—or, at least, portions of what happened. Apparently, the only person who knows chapter-and-verse is my husband, and he's not telling.

CHAPTER 21

"I just wanted to let the boyos play at the park," Doyle complained to Maguire that night. "Is that so much to ask? But instead I'm hit with brick-bat after brick-bat of shockin' news."

"I'm afraid there are more brick-bats to come," said her ghostly Job's comforter.

"Well that's just crackin' *grand*. And meanwhile Acton is usin' heaps of aristo-speak—which is what he does whenever he's being very careful with his words. It's drivin' me mad."

"He has to be careful," the reporter agreed. "He's very surprised that you know as much as you do."

"Aye," Doyle agreed. "He said he's keepin' everythin' a secret because he's not 'acquitted well'—and there's a dose of aristo-speak for you—but I don't have the sense that he regrets a single thing. He's steeled to the teeth."

"Yes," the reporter agreed. "Not unexpected."

"Actually, it is," she disagreed thoughtfully. "He doesn't

handle it well, when I've been hurt—usually I've my work cut out, havin' to settle him down. Faith, I'm that surprised he hasn't shut himself up with a bottle o' scotch, and have to be walked-back from the ledge."

"Perhaps that is yet to come," the ghost suggested. "After his ordeal is over."

She looked up at him in surprise. "But—that's what I don't understand; isn't his ordeal already over?"

Maguire pointed out, "So far, the scotch is safe."

"Aye, that. Mayhap this one was such a corker that it broke his usual pattern—after all, he was brawlin' like a dockman and browbeatin' nurses, of all things. Acton's not one to browbeat service-people, and so it just goes to show that he must have been mighty shook-up, poor man."

Reminded, she added, "And speakin' of such, one of my nurses has disappeared—did you know? She'd a married beau, though, which always makes the CID narrow its eyes."

"A familiar trope, in crime stories," he agreed.

She knit her brow as she contemplated the ghost. "Although the beau's gone missin' too—and he was known to be somethin' of a chouser. Faith, the whole thing smells like Friday's fish on Monday morn. Did you know him? A reporter named Bradford Song."

"No, I did not have that pleasure."

Doyle heard the disapproval in his tone and nodded. "Apparently, he didn't know when to pull-in his horns, and Acton thinks he may have gone and rattled the wrong cage."

"Yes," Maguire agreed. "Mr. Song definitely rattled the wrong cage."

Doyle blinked in surprise. "You know what's happened to him, then? Was he tryin' to muscle someone?"

"He was. Only he's the one who wound-up getting muscled."

She nodded in a knowing fashion. "We call that a preemption-murder, at the CID; some little fish is causin' trouble for the bigger fish and so the little fish is taken-out—bam—and all problems are solved."

"Rather like squashing an annoying little fly."

The words hung in the air, and—reminded of Maguire's own take-down, long ago—Doyle offered, "Brings back bad memories, I suppose."

The ghost bowed his head. "There are some definite similarities."

But she protested, "I wouldn't say you were a chouser, Mr. Maguire; instead you were—you were a bit misguided, mayhap."

"You are being kind, Officer Doyle."

"Not a'tall," she insisted stoutly. "You meant well—you badgered people because you thought you were helpin' the wrongfully charged. This Song fellow was all puffed-up and makin' threats to serve his own purposes—it's the next thing to blackmail."

"He was not a good newsman," Maguire agreed. "And I thank you for the vote of confidence."

Thoughtfully, Doyle mused, "So; to solve his murder I suppose I need only look into Song's latest articles to see who might have taken umbrum—umbram—"

"Umbrage," the ghost provided.

"Aye—thank you. It shouldn't be too hard to get a list of potential suspects." Thinking this over, she knit her brow. "But if Bradford Song was killed for rattlin' the wrong cage, why then was Colleen Cadigan killed? She's not a brashy reporter."

Maguire smiled. "Very good."

Doyle looked up at him. "Very good, what?"

"A very good question."

Into the silence, Doyle ventured, "We were thinkin' that mayhap she saw somethin' she shouldn't have—she was what we call an inadvertent witness. Or she was with Song when he was taken-out—just happened to be in the wrong place at the wrong time."

"I'd suggest you find out."

Blowing out a breath, she agreed. "Aye; I need to find out why Colleen Cadigan's dead—if she is—and whether her death is related to Song's preemption-murder. It can't be a coincidence."

But the ghost revealed, "It is a coincidence, actually. A very fortunate coincidence."

Surprised, she stared at him. "Doesn't seem very fortunate for poor Nurse Cadigan, I must say. And Acton doesn't believe in coincidences—not when it comes to homicide cases."

"This one's indeed a coincidence," he assured her. "Or at least it was, until it wasn't."

There was a small silence. "You're talkin' in circles," she ventured. "I haven't the smallest inklin'."

"You will—I have faith in you. Keep digging, and follow the story."

She made a wry mouth. "My husband doesn't want me to, Mr. Maguire, which makes for a rugged hill to climb."

"All the more reason. Who would know the facts?"

Thoughtfully, Doyle mused, "Savoie knows somethin'—but he's not budgin'."

"No. And so, you must search elsewhere."

Doyle counted on her fingers. "Rachel Anderson. Williams." She paused. "Reynolds," she added thoughtfully. "I think Reynolds knows somethin'."

"Very good. Anyone else?"

"Seamus Riordan, I suppose. He was there—or at least, he was there when they fished me out of the river. But he's a witness under wraps, at present, so I don't know how I can contact him without Acton's knowin' about it."

"Right. Anyone else?"

Slowly, Doyle shook her head. "I don't think so."

The ghost tilted his head in mild disagreement.

"Who?" she asked with a hint of impatience. "I wouldn't know, since I'm the one who was conked-out, remember? You should be the one who's tellin' me."

"No, you've forgot someone, but not to worry—you'll get there. You've done very well so far—I'm very impressed."

"I feel like I'm playin' blind man's bluff," Doyle confessed, somewhat mollified by his praise. "Nothin' seems to be addin' up."

"Right," the ghost agreed. "Which is exactly how he wants it."

Doyle nodded, since this much seemed evident; Acton had a scheme underway—according to Maguire he was setting a trap—but she hadn't the foggiest notion for who—whom?—he was setting it; all the blacklegs were dead or scattered. "I need to speak with that reporter again—Rachel Anderson. She seems to know a lot about all this."

"Good idea."

Alive to the nuance in his tone, he ventured, "I don't think you're very happy with her, Mr. Maguire."

"That doesn't matter. Follow the story, wherever it leads."

Suddenly struck, she said, "You know, I should try to speak with Mrs. Song. I'll bet she knows a thing or two, but I've no idea how I can swing it."

"Now, there's your best lead yet," he declared in an encouraging tone.

Doyle blinked. "But she didn't kill her husband—right? I thought you said his was a preemption-murder."

But she was not to hear an answer because she found that she had awakened, and was staring at the ceiling in her bedroom.

CHAPTER 22

She was so beautiful, when the air was brisk and her cheeks were pink.

After they'd returned from walking Edward to school the next morning, Acton excused himself to go to his office and Miss Cherry left with Tommy to go feed the ducks, which gave Doyle a few quiet minutes to think about her dream.

She settled-in at the kitchen table, idly gazing out the windows as she tried to make some sense of it all. Mainly, it seemed that Maguire was giving her a call-to-action to speak to a list of witnesses—and one witness that she was overlooking, apparently—but this was a tall order for someone who was off-the-clock and wrapped in cotton-wool. Nevertheless, Maguire was shown to give good advice—and after all, she'd nothing better to do; at least until Acton was reinstated and she was cleared for duty.

Of course, she might be called-upon to testify about that disaster-day if the artwork case was ever revived—now, there was something she was not looking forward to. Presumably, everything having to do with the London aspect of the case was on hold, though, with Kirken having fled and the other two defendants murdered. But once they found Kirken, she'd probably have to be a prime witness alongside Seamus Riordan, since she'd seen the evidence too, before the fire destroyed it.

Faith, but she'd hate to have to re-live that horror-show. Mayhap Kirken would realize it was hopeless and plead guilty so as to avoid a public trial. Or they wouldn't find him at all—he was probably hiding out on the Continent, somewhere, living in terror that he'd be the next preemption-murder. Which would be a good riddance and nothing less than he deserved.

But her mind was wandering, and she should try to stick to the topic at hand, which was trying to puzzle-out what her dream meant. Maguire seemed to be steering her toward a collection of different things; the Song-Cadigan case, which was connected—somehow?—to the donnybrook at the hospital. He'd said it was all a coincidence until it wasn't—which made little sense. The only link seemed to be that one of her nurses was having an affair with the famous reporter, and was probably dead as a result, poor lady.

Why was that important? It truly seemed a coincidence—and a side-note that the fair Doyle would never have even known about, save that she'd gone over to discover what she could about the donnybrook at the hospital.

Which—come to think of it—was nothing; the nurses on staff hadn't a clue, and she was no further along in finding out what had happened than when she'd first begun. Well, save she now knew both Williams and Savoie were involved—now, there was an unlikely pairing, and it made for a couple more handsome men for the lusty nurses to admire.

Oh, she suddenly realized, lifting her head; there's the significant thing that I'd forgot; the nurse had referred to my security-man as being tall, dark and handsome but it wasn't Trenton and it wasn't my husband. And that description doesn't fit Williams or Savoie.

With a knit brow, she considered this. Who would come to see her at the hospital who'd fit such a description? Not Rolph. Not Reynolds—he wasn't particularly tall or handsome, and was unlikely to inspire lust in nurse's hearts.

Her gaze rested on the butler—who was doing an inventory in the pantry—and she was reminded of a something the ghost had said. "What's a 'trope,' Reynolds? That's a good word—it's rather like 'brusque,' which is another good word—sounds exactly like what it means."

The servant straightened up to gaze at her in surprise. "Who was being brusque, madam?"

"Never you mind; just tell me what a trope is."

Crossing his arms, the servant considered this. "A trope in literature is something that is familiar and reoccurring. Oftentimes, characters are tropes."

Frowning, she gazed at him. "Not followin', my friend."

The butler explained, "For example, the evil genius is a trope you often see. Or the reluctant hero."

Doyle's brow cleared. "Oh—*that's* what he meant. There's a home-wreckin' brasser in this story and she met a bad end. It *is* a trope."

Warming to the theme, Reynolds added, "The charming rogue. The flawed champion."

"The wicked stepmother—you see that one a lot," Doyle observed thoughtfully. "Sometimes she's a mother-in-law."

"The staunch supporter," the servant suggested.

Doyle knit her brow. "Is that the same as the trusty sidekick?"

"Indeed, madam."

"Well, there's a lot of tropes in criminal cases too," Doyle informed him. "You see the same patterns again and again. There's the smart-woman-who-stupidly-falls-for-the-wrong-man; been seein' a lot of that one lately."

"The misguided heroine," Reynolds clarified. "Although she is soon to see the error of her ways."

A bit sadly, Doyle shook her head. "This time, she didn't."

"Oh? Then you must not be reading Austen, madam."

"I'm not readin' anythin', Reynolds, save for those occasions when I'm readin' Acton the Riot Act—fancy his gettin' himself a black eye."

The servant offered no reply to this remark, but instead bent to re-address the pantry shelves whilst Doyle eyed him thoughtfully.

At this juncture, Acton came up the stairs and walked over to the table, cradling her head in his hands to kiss her brow before sitting beside her. "Have you been speaking with anyone about your recovery, Kathleen? There is an article in the *London World News* today that claims you are fully recovered and doing well. It cites an anonymous source."

"I'm the source," Doyle readily confessed. "When I went to have lunch with Lizzie, a reporter recognized me."

After congratulating herself for thinking of a version of events which hewed fairly close to the truth, she then decided to add, "I should phone to thank the woman; she seemed very nice, and she could have revealed that I was at a fancy tea shop —which would have been truly embarrassin'—but she didn't."

"Only be careful what you say, Kathleen," he warned gently.

"Aye—I'm a gabbler, and no bones about it. But even if I gabble about somethin' I oughtn't you can always call the publisher and ask him to scrub it." This, because such a thing had actually happened, and on more than one occasion.

"Let's not test it, if you please."

She laughed and pulled him toward her for a kiss. "You're whistlin' in the wind, my friend; I'm forever sayin' the wrong thing to the wrong person."

"All part of your charm," he declared, even though she could sense that he'd ambiguous feelings on the subject.

"While I'm at it, I should put in a good word for you, Michael; boost your chances of gettin' off suspension."

"I imagine this inauspicious situation will very soon resolve itself."

"Now, there's a dose of aristo-speak," she noted.

"An unfortunate habit," he replied with a smile. "Forgive me."

"I wouldn't change a single thing," she declared loyally, whilst mentally congratulating herself for creating an excuse to call the reporter without raising his radar—faith, there were times when she could be just as wily as he was.

And this, in turn, reminded her that she'd also managed to brainstorm a plausible excuse to speak to another witness on Maguire's list. "You know, Michael; I wonder if we should go interview Bradford Song's wife. It would be interestin' to see whether she knows about him and the nurse, and whether she's willin' to lie about it."

He replied, "A good thought, but we are not active-duty, at present."

"I was thinkin' that we'd not go in a professional capacity—instead we'd go hat-in-hand to the benefactress. We can try to talk her into supportin' Sunshine Bakery, which would have the added benefit of keepin' Savoie's mitts out of the government till. It's a valid excuse, and meanwhile we can see what's-what with respect to her missin' husband."

He was silent—with a jolt of hope, she could see that his

interest was caught—and so she added, "We've got nothin' better to do, and I've a feelin' it may be important to speak with her." Remembering Maguire's words, she added, "There's somethin' here that was a coincidence, until it wasn't."

Since her husband knew to pay close attention whenever the wife of his bosom had one of her "feelings," this seemed to turn the trick. "Very well; I will arrange for it."

He rose, and walked over to the windows to make the call as she watched him thoughtfully. She'd the sense that he was only humoring her—he truly didn't think they'd discover anything useful. But meanwhile, Maguire seemed to think that Mrs. Song was her best lead yet—it was all very interesting.

"Would you care for a scone, madam?"

She smiled up at Reynolds. "Only if I get to dunk it in strong coffee."

The butler threw a quick, admonishing glance Acton's way since the master-of-the-house tended to look askance at coffee-drinking during pregnancy but the butler-of-the-house would nevertheless slip the mistress-of-the-house the occasional half-cup.

She sighed. "Never mind; I suppose I'll have ginger tea, instead. On ice, please."

"Very good, madam."

She turned her attention back to Acton, who was speaking on the phone and admiring the view with a casual hand in his pocket—an unusual stance for him, especially in his usually-busy mornings. Doyle watched him and thought, he's seems perfectly content to leave everything in limbo—his suspension, my medical leave, the artwork case—nothing's on a deadline because he's waiting for something to happen. Maguire mentioned a coming ordeal, but I can't think of what it could be; it certainly seems as though the ordeal has already taken place, and I'm left to piece it all together after the fact. It's all very strange.

"Tomorrow morning," Acton announced as he returned to the table. "We have an appointment at ten."

"Excellent," she said. "Can we arrest her, if she confesses to stranglin' her wretched husband?"

"Perhaps not," he replied with a smile. "We shouldn't court an entrapment defense."

"Ah, good point."

"If you will excuse me? I should check-in with my caseload."

He headed toward the stairway, and she called out, "When's your hearin', again?"

"Soon," he assured her, as he departed down the stairs.

Such an annoying gombeen, she thought. "Don't forget to have McGonigal come over soon, too," she called out as a parting shot.

And—since she was already firing-off shots—she decided to address Reynolds, as he approached with her ginger tea. "You know, Reynolds, I think Savoie filched Tanya Denisovich's pearl necklace but I can't figure-out when the two of them were in the same place."

Ah, now there was a direct hit; Reynolds set her drink down rather abruptly and was carefully trying to hide his flare of acute alarm.

Doyle eyed him. "Tell me what you know about this, my friend."

In an apologetic tone, the servant replied, "I am afraid I am not at liberty to say, madam."

Crossly, Doyle complained, "It can't be good for my poor noggin to have to do all this bird-doggin'. Faith, what I wouldn't give for a bit more plain-speakin' from any one of the lot of you."

Fortunately for Reynolds, he was granted a reprieve from coming up with an response because the Concierge buzzed, and he hurried over to answer the intercom.

"Mr. Williams is below," the butler announced. "He is dropping off the gloves you left behind at the tea house."

Well, here's something, thought Doyle, who'd forgot to wear gloves in the first place, when she'd gone to meet with Lizzie. Apparently, one of my witnesses is willing to come to me, for a change. "Tell him I'll be straight down," she informed the servant, and then headed for the door with no further ado.

CHAPTER 23

Good; it appeared the bait had been taken. In two days, he would see an end to it.

Doyle emerged from the lift, and saw that Williams was waiting by the lobby's entry door. "Ho," she greeted him. "What's up?"

"I thought I'd come by to see if you'd like to take a little walk."

"I already took a walk this mornin'," she groused.

"Let's go," he replied in a firm tone, a hand on her back as he steered her out the door. "I'll buy you a coffee."

"Fine, then. Let me borrow your coat."

He paused to comply with this request, and glanced over his shoulder as he did so. "Where's Trenton?"

"Trenton's with Miss Cherry and Tommy over at the pond. What's afoot, my friend?" He seemed a bit grave, but she didn't have the sense that there was any sort of emergency unfolding.

They emerged onto the pavement and walked a few paces in

silence; apparently, he wanted to be well-clear of any chance of being overheard. "I wanted to talk to you about the Bradford Song case."

She raised her brows. "Oh? Anythin' new?"

"No. Instead, I was wondering why you seem so interested."

Annoyed, Doyle retorted, "I'm interested because everyone's tryin' to keep me in the dark and I don't appreciate it *a'tall*."

He was silent for a moment as they walked along. "What makes you think that?"

She took a breath to calm herself down; no need to take out her frustrations on Williams, who could always be depended upon to be solidly in her corner—a staunch supporter, if there ever was one. "Acton gave me some flim-flam about why you were handlin' the Song missin' persons case, but it seemed mighty weak sauce. And then, when Munoz and I figured-out that Song was a plausible suspect for the nurse's murder, Acton shuttles the file off to you quick-as-a-cat."

He said nothing as they walked along, and she raised her palms. "So; can you blame me? In the usual course of affairs when such a thing happens, it's because you and Acton are handlin' somethin' under-the-table and you want to keep whatever's happenin' from pryin' eyes. But that doesn't make a lot of sense, in this instance; if this reporter's managed to brash himself into a preemption-murder, wouldn't we want to know whose toes he stepped on, so we can go after 'em?"

Williams continued silent—controlling himself very carefully, the man was—and so she added, "Not to mention that we should try to bring justice to my poor nurse—even though her death muddies the water a bit, as to motive. But that's all the more reason to follow the proper protocols, and pursue what leads we have. Both Song's and Cadigan's electronics revealed that the lights went out after they met a mystery person at a Hampstead park." Glancing up at him, she decided to add, "It gives me flashbacks to the Maguire murders, save that Maguire is dead as a door-nail."

Williams lifted his gaze to the upcoming intersection. "I'm afraid I can't tell you much. But I came over to ask that you drop it, Kath. You're on leave, anyway, and believe me, we would all be better off."

This was of interest, mainly because she'd a ghost who was directing her to do just the opposite. "D'you want the Song-Cadigan situation to go cold, for some reason? Is that why Acton's pulled you in—he wants you to put a lid on it?"

This was a shrewd guess, but his answer was not what she'd been expecting. "No, I am putting a case together at full speed and we do have a suspect."

She stared at him in surprise. "Oh. For heaven's sake, Thomas—why didn't you just say so?"

He blew out a breath, as they waited for the crossing light. "Because we're keeping it quiet, for now. That's why I'd like you to stand down, Kath; it would be for the best."

Doubtfully, she advised, "I'm not very good at stayin' away from things, Thomas."

"Right. But in this case, it's important."

She ventured, "Did Acton put you up to givin' me this warnin'?"

"No—I'm here on my own. But he'd say the same thing; it would be for the best if you drop it."

Annoyed all over again, she drew her brows down. "Shouldn't I be the judge of that, Thomas Williams?"

As though coming to a decision, he said bluntly, "There's a personal aspect for me, this time around."

This was true, and she stared at him in dismay. "Holy

Mother, Thomas; don't tell me you were havin' an affair with Cadigan too?"

"No—nothing like that." He met her eyes very seriously. "You just have to trust me, Kath. I can't say why, only that it's important."

A bit stricken that she'd caused him to be so grave, she took his arm as they began walking forward again. "Aye, then; I'll needle you no more. But can you throw me a bone and tell me who socked you one?"

Surprisingly, his mood lightened somewhat, as they approached the entrance to the coffee franchise. "You wouldn't believe it, even if I told you."

She slid her gaze to his. "You're forgettin' that I would, as a matter of fact."

"Oh—right." He paused as though thinking about it, and then disclosed, "Sir Vikili."

She stared at him, completely astonished. "*Sir Vikili* was throwin' punches? Mother a' Mercy, but this must have been some dust-up. Is he the one who clocked Acton, too?"

"I don't think so—I'm not sure who did."

The light dawned, and suddenly Doyle realized the identity of the tall, dark and handsome man. "What was Sir Vikili doin' at the hospital in the first place?"

Startled, his eyes met hers and she was suddenly reminded that she wasn't supposed to know that the donnybrook was at the hospital—her wretched, wretched tongue.

"Leave it alone, Kath—I'm begging you."

Chastened by the seriousness of his tone, she nodded and resolved to say nothing more to him on the subject.

CHAPTER 24

When Doyle came back from her coffee-excursion, she teetered on the edge of confronting Acton about it. It was in her nature to pull things out into the open, and she always thought that this was the best tack to take with her naturally-secretive husband. In a strange way, she'd the sense that it eased his mind; he'd learned from long experience that he could trust her, and he was one who didn't trust anyone.

Her scalp prickled, and she thought—yes, it's true. Her husband might trust Williams to some extent—along with the faithful retainers from Trestles, like Hudson—but all in all, he trusted no one completely save for the fair Doyle. Or mayhap it wasn't as much that he trusted her as she was the center of his world, and if she decided to lead him to his doom he'd willingly go.

It was a weighty responsibility, and it led to situations such as this one—her impulse was to confront him on this Song-Cadigan matter and discover what had spooked Williams, but instead, careful handling was probably the order of the day; she needed to find out more, first. She'd been thrown a bit by Williams' dire warning because it was almost as though—almost as though Williams was afraid of Acton.

Oh, she realized, rather startled; that's it—Williams is afraid of Acton and it stems, somehow, from Song and Cadigan and the events leading up to the mysterious donnybrook at the hospital. But why would this be? Did Williams cross Acton, somehow? Or mayhap the man had got himself into trouble—it had happened before, where Acton had been forced to step-in and pull Williams' coals from the fire.

But that explanation didn't seem to fit this particular instance, since Acton had clearly enlisted Williams as his henchman—same as he always did, when he needed something done under-the-radar.

Although apparently, it wasn't the usual situation where everything was going to be swept under the rug; this time, they were pursuing a suspect—which was the strangest thing of all; if Acton and Williams knew who'd killed the two lovers, why was it such a secret? And why would Williams be so unnerved about it?

She frowned, considering this. From what he'd hinted, it was a personal matter—even though he'd been telling the truth when he'd said he wasn't having an affair with the nurse. But nonetheless, it *must* have to do with Cadigan—that seemed to be the only possible link; Cadigan was a nurse at the hospital, and Williams was at the donnybrook at the aforesaid hospital. As was Sir Vikili, who'd apparently taken the opportunity to have a go at Williams—but one strange puzzle-piece at a time, she'd have to come back to that one later.

Her thoughts were interrupted by Reynolds, who discreetly

placed a half-cup of coffee before her—much-appreciated even though she'd just had a half-cup with Williams. After debating for a moment, she lifted the cup—she should at least take a few sips, since the servant was risking Acton's displeasure in bringing her the forbidden brew. Although perhaps Reynolds was golden, too—she'd the niggling sense that the butler and Acton were holding a secret, betwixt them.

"You know, Reynolds," she said aloud; "Williams has got himself banged-up, just like Acton. I wonder if they were havin' a go at each other."

Nonplussed, the servant offered, "Such a thing would be very unexpected, madam."

Her gaze rested on the butler over the lip of her coffee-cup. "No more unexpected than the two of them takin' a blow from someone else, when they're both top o' the trees in hand-to-hand. And where was Trenton, when the fists were flyin'? So much for his bein' a staunch supporter."

"I do not know, madam."

This was true—which was not surprising if the only one who knew what had happened was Acton. Although there was another witness in the knows-a-lot category, and so Doyle decided there was no time like the present to ring-up Rachel Anderson.

The phone call was sent to voice-mail, and then, when Doyle identified herself, Anderson readily picked up. "I didn't know it was you," she apologized.

"I wanted to thank you for the mention in the *World News*," Doyle said. "Any chance you're free for a cup of coffee?"

"Oh—now?"

"If you wouldn't mind. And if you'll fetch the coffee, I can meet you at the park gate on Grosvenor Street." Doyle checked the time. "It won't take long; I have to go pick-up my son afterward, and it's on the way."

"Right. How do you like your coffee?

"Strong," said Doyle, and mentally apologized to baby Mary.

CHAPTER 25

Doyle pondered giving her husband the head's up about this latest escape from her cotton-wool, but instead compromised by ringing-up Trenton. "I'm headed over to the park, Trenton, just so you know. Acton's in his office, so it will just be me."

"Very good, ma'am."

Doyle rang off, and then contemplated the mobile for a moment, suddenly struck by the possibility that mayhap the other witness Maguire referred to was Trenton. Trenton must know a thing or two about the donnybrook—mainly how he managed to fail in his duties to such an extent that Acton got punched in the face. But even if he were a witness to these strange and unexpected events, there was no way Trenton would tell her a blessed thing; instead, he'd immediately squeak to Acton that she'd been asking.

And so, with Trenton walking at a discreet distance behind her, Doyle set out for the designated park gate and then loitered for a few minutes until she sighted Rachel Anderson, coming along the pavement with a coffee carrier.

"Thanks," said Doyle, as the two women moved to sit down on the nearest bench. "I wanted to thank you for your article, and give you an update on the Song case."

Emanating anxiety, the other woman immediately lowered her coffee. "Oh? What have you found out?"

"Not a lot—which is never a good thing, when you're dealin' with someone who's got credit cards and electronics. I think you may have to brace yourself for bad news."

Sadly, the other girl nodded. "Yes. It does seem as though it's been too long to have heard nothing."

Doyle sipped her coffee, and then casually asked, "Were you at the hospital, when they had the donnybrook? I was surprised you knew about it—they're keepin' it very quiet."

"No—I wasn't there, but Bradford had a source. He didn't want to tell me much—he said that even if he told me, I wouldn't believe it."

Behaving as though she knew more than she did, Doyle nodded sagely. "Aye—there were some desperate criminals involved."

But Anderson only raised her brows in surprise. "Were there? It sounded as though a fight broke out because someone wanted to move you out of critical care. Who would try to do such a thing?"

Not a clue, thought Doyle, completely bewildered. Acton had indeed moved her to Trestles, but it was hard to believe that he'd engage in a fistfight over it—and as her husband, he'd have every right to clear her out. Not to mention that it didn't explain why Sir Vikili and Williams were tangling—the whole tale was completely unbelievable, save that it had actually happened and her husband was taking great care to cover it up.

Thinking of another potential source of information, Doyle asked, "Was Song writin' up a story about it? Any chance that I could look at his notes?"

But the other woman only shook her head. "I don't think so—he would have asked me to help him write it."

So; as it turned out, there wasn't much to be gleaned from Ms. Anderson after all, but the discussion was not yet finished and Doyle mentally girded her loins. "I want to give you a bit of a scoldin', so brace yourself."

Understandably surprised, Anderson raised her eyebrows. "You do?"

"Aye; you're a trope—and I think that when you're a trope you don't always realize it, and so it's left to me to tell you. You're a misguided heroine—or more accurately, a smart woman who's been stupid when it comes to love. We see a lot of them, unfortunately, and usually they're cryin' in the interview room, unable to believe what a mess they've got themselves into."

Anderson stared at her for a moment and Doyle had the feeling she was trying to decide whether to disclaim and laugh it off. But instead, the young woman bent her head and examined the coffee cup in her lap.

Doyle continued, "Song was the sort of man who used women to advance his own career."

"Oh—I know," Anderson admitted rather defensively, as she readily met Doyle's gaze. "He used to joke about it with me—that women would tell him things they wouldn't dare tell anyone else."

"Well, that's not all he did. I know for a fact he was havin' an affair with a nurse over at the hospital and promisin' that he'd marry her."

The other woman's mouth fell open as she stared at Doyle. "*What?*"

Doyle nodded, and thought she may as well mention, "And meanwhile, he's married." Not that it seemed to matter to our Ms. Anderson, here, but it mattered to Doyle.

The girl's lips began to tremble and she ducked her head, rapidly blinking back tears.

"I'm sorry," Doyle offered rather gently. "I imagine he was usin' you, too."

Anderson took a long breath and admitted, "He had me write some of his stories, and put them under his byline. I knew it wasn't right, but he said I'd be doing him a huge favor because he was so busy."

"There you go," said Doyle. "A chouser, through-and-through."

In a low voice, the other woman admitted, "I thought—I thought he rather fancied me. It was so—so amazing; that someone like him would fancy someone like me."

Faith—know *that* feeling, thought Doyle. "All the same, you've got to stay true to yourself, lass."

Discreetly, the other girl wiped her eyes with her fingertips. "I'm glad you told me, Officer Doyle. I know it's awkward, and you didn't have to."

"Well, we're not done just yet, because—chouser or no—I intend to bring him some justice. To that end, I'd like to know what he was coverin' lately; he may have overturned the wrong stone and that's why he's disappeared."

Anderson nodded, thinking about this. "He's made some enemies," she admitted. "He just laughed about it, though—thought it was funny, more than anything."

"Any recent enemies?"

Slowly, Anderson shook her head. "Not that I knew; he's been very keen on the Torrance case—the mercy killing."

Doyle nodded, "Aye—so I heard. He was takin' the side of the husband."

"Yes. He wanted me to write an article on the subject every day, and put it under his byline. He felt it was very unjust, the way the police wanted to arrest the man for murder."

This seemed unconnected to Doyle's concerns, but—knowing that Williams was skeptical about the husband's motives in that case—she offered, "It's never a good idea to try to sway people to suit your own notions—not before you're acquainted with all the facts, leastways. It may have been before your time, but there was a reporter named Kevin Maguire who got himself into a spot of trouble, thinkin' he could shift people's opinions."

"Kevin Maguire was my mentor," Anderson said.

There was a small pause. "Was he indeed?"

The other woman nodded. "When I first interned at the *World News*. I don't care what people say—he was a good newsman."

"No argument, here," said Doyle.

Since the mercy-killing case seemed unrelated, Doyle concluded, "Well, please let me know if you hear that Song was makin' any enemies, lately—at this point, I'm happy to hear even rumors."

"I will," Anderson agreed. "I'd like to bring him some justice, too."

But Doyle warned, "Don't you dare mourn the man, like that woman in that famous story."

Her companion couldn't help but smile. "Which famous story is that?"

"The one with the dead lass in a boat, all mopey because her stupid knight was a chouser."

"Elaine?" the other guessed.

"That's the one. That's an even worse trope than yours—promise me you'll not do yourself in over the likes of a man like Bradford Song."

Still smiling, the other girl ducked her head. "I won't. I'm too ashamed."

"Well, you're young, and no real harm done," Doyle offered in a worldly tone, even though she'd wasn't much older than our Ms. Anderson, here—not to mention that she'd been miles more naïve, when Acton had first thrown her across his saddle-bow. "Lesson learned."

CHAPTER 26

This was unexpected.

Doyle looked up to see Trenton, walking along the path in front of the bench and giving her a quick glance as he did so. Responding, she raised a finger—meaning all was well—and then saw that Acton was hovering on the other side of the hedgerow, no doubt wondering if he could approach and interrupt whatever was going forward.

With a smile, Doyle rose and gestured to him. "Here comes my husband—I'll have to cut it short. Thanks for the coffee."

"Thank you, Officer Doyle."

Doyle then introduced a rather flustered Anderson to Acton, who nodded in his polite, aristocratic way even as he took Doyle's elbow and guided her away. After a few paces, he asked, "And who was that?"

"The reporter with the *London World News*—the one I saw when I went to the tea room."

Acton glanced up at the pathway ahead. "Trenton tells me there were some tears involved."

Doyle had to smile, thinking of her husband's reaction when Trenton decided to inform him that his wife was making a strange woman cry in the park across the way. "Aye—I gave her a piece of advice. She was in love with Song, foolish thing, and I told her that she'd better things to do than yearn after a blackleg. She's a misguided heroine, and so I had to show her the error of her ways—just like in those books that Reynolds talks about."

There was a small pause. "This is fascinating," her husband said in all sincerity.

"Aye, my mind's a rabbit-warren—takes more than a little knock, to put it out of commission."

"Anything useful gleaned?"

"No. I asked if Song had made any enemies lately, but she didn't seem to think so. She said he was up-in-arms about the Torrance mercy-killin' case—was havin' our Ms. Anderson write articles about it under his name—which just goes to show how foolish women can be."

"Not you," he offered with a small smile.

"Fah—I'm the pattern-card for foolishness, husband; I married you without havin' the first clue what I was in for, and thank God fastin' it's all turned out well." She paused. "Mostly, anyways."

There was a small silence as they walked a few paces. "You are unhappy with me, Kathleen?"

"I am. Williams is afraid, and Williams doesn't scare easy."

Almost immediately he assured her, "Williams has nothing to fear."

"Good. If Williams did a bunk, I'd no trusty supporters left, save Reynolds."

"I am your trusty supporter," he protested.

"No—you're the flawed champion in this story, and it's an epic one. Talk about rabbit-warrens, this you-and-me tale takes the palm."

He started chuckling and rather surprised—he was one who rarely laughed—she glanced up at him. "What?"

He stopped, right there on the pathway, to draw her into his arms; holding her tightly against him. "I am so happy you are alive."

"Me, too," she replied, her voice muffled against his chest. "Although I didn't realize it was close."

"It was close," he said.

She lifted her chin to address him—not easy, since he was holding her so tightly. "Yet you'll not give me chapter-and-verse?"

"No." He released her to walk forward again, arm-in-arm. "I don't even like to think about it."

With sympathy, she squeezed his waist. "Sorry I gave you such a rough go, Michael."

He gazed upward at the tree branches. "A very trying time."

Since he seemed to have let down his guard a bit, she teetered on the edge of asking him why Sir Vikili had belted Williams, but then backed off; if he didn't wish to talk about it she should respect that—not to mention that she might land Williams back in the soup if she revealed that he'd been telling tales.

And more than anything else, she had the sure sense that her husband was in a vulnerable state—after all, a public embrace was very much out-of-keeping. Couple this with the unhappy piano-music and it all added-up to the inescapable conclusion that he was very uneven, beneath all this calmness.

Which shouldn't be a surprise; she'd a near-brush, after all, and meanwhile—according to Maguire—he was trying to orchestrate something under-the-radar so that she wouldn't be aware, even though there seemed to be no reason for such secrecy. An ordeal, of all things—which was an odd choice of word; you'd think nothing save for his wife would be ordeal-worthy, in Acton's world, and his wife was doing just fine.

But Maguire seemed to know of which he spoke, so instead of scolding the man like an archwife, she should be trying to ease his worries—no easy task, since she seemed no closer to any answers than she was when Maguire had first made his ghostly appearance.

On impulse, she lifted her face to his. "I'd defend you to the last yard, too, Michael," she assured him. "Even though I'm not Trestles-folk."

Understandably surprised, he bent his head close to hers. "I appreciate it. Is there something I should know?"

She smiled. "No—I just thought I'd say. I may complain that you always want to wrap me in cotton-wool, but I know it's only because you love me so. And I love you so right back, and just as fiercely; I don't say it near enough."

"You don't have to say," he replied, and kissed her forehead. "Not to me."

CHAPTER 27

"It's all very symmetrical," the ghost said that night, a thread of humor in his voice. "You once gave me a scolding on a park bench."

Doyle smiled. "Our Ms. Anderson's a good egg, I think; she was taken-in, and I'm sure she's not the only one. People like Song are very good at takin' advantage a little bit at a time, and rachetin' it up slowly so that by the time you finally feel uneasy about it, it's that much harder to say no."

"Yes. A master manipulator."

Doyle ventured, "Is Anderson the friend you're doin' a favor for?"

"No," he replied. "I was assigned as her mentor when she was an intern. We have little in common."

She regarded him for a moment. "I still think—friend or no—that you care enough to try to straighten her out a bit."

"Perhaps."

Doyle sighed. "I wish I could straighten-out my poor husband; there's somethin' here that's makin' me worry—somethin' rather grim. He may seem calm, but it's only because he's steeled himself."

"Yes."

She made a sound of sympathy. "The poor man's had a rough go—rougher than mine, actually, since I don't remember anythin'. He'd a lot to handle, what with me bein' hurt, and then his goin' after Elliott and Denisovich like the seven bowls of wrath—not to mention Kirken was tryin' to lock him up and take hold of me in the hospital. Faith, when you think about it, Kirken had the most to answer for, but he's the one who managed to evade Acton's wrath and slip the net, somehow—"

Suddenly struck, she stilled. "Oh—oh, that's it, I think. Acton and Williams are goin' after Kirken. Williams is buildin' a case to frame Kirken for murderin' the other two—it would fit; the magistrate would have the motive, because he'd want to keep the others from testifyin' against him."

"Very good," said Maguire approvingly.

Blowing out a breath, Doyle exclaimed, "Mother a' Mercy, but I can't believe it's taken me this long to figure it out. Acton may be the grand master at coverin' his tracks, but he's also the grand master at turnin' the tables, and he's done exactly this sort of thing many a time against someone who tried to cross him—faith, the man could probably do it in his sleep. He's doin' a frame-up—just like he did with Sir Stephen, his awful cousin. He'll weave a spider-web—very calm and patient—until there's no possible escape, and nary a hint that would lead back to him as the cause of the frame-up."

"Exactly."

She made a wry mouth. "Small wonder he doesn't want me to know what he's up to—and small wonder he wanted to keep me out of the arena, and locked-away at Trestles—I always try to throw a wrench in all his vengeance-plans." She paused, and then admitted, "Although most times his vengeance-plans are wife-proof."

"Nevertheless, it stands you in good stead. He has to be more flexible than he'd like, because you tend to counter his plans."

"Aye; it's that yin-and-yams thing."

The ghost smiled slightly. "There you go."

She nodded. "I do pull him off-track; only see how he couldn't help givin' me a bear hug—right there on the park pathway. That's not his trope a'tall."

"His trope is brooding and dangerous," the ghost said in a dry tone.

But Doyle shook her head. "No—not dangerous to me, leastways. And I know him better than anyone."

"I know him better than most," the ghost countered.

This was true; Maguire had managed to piece together an exposé of Acton's many misdeeds and was about to put it to print when he changed his mind, after becoming friends with the fair Doyle.

Diplomatically, she offered, "Well, I suppose we can at least agree that he's not as dangerous as he used to be—and not as broodin', either."

Now it was Maguire's turn to be diplomatic. "A matter of perspective, perhaps."

Doyle sighed. "There's no pleasin' you, Mr. Maguire."

"On the contrary, I am very pleased—you've pieced together much of the story."

But Doyle wasn't as optimistic. "I still haven't learned much about the donnybrook, though—nor how Song and Cadigan fit in. Williams wasn't much help, and neither was Rachel Anderson. We're going to see Mrs. Song tomorrow and—unless she's miles more helpful than they were—there's only the mystery witness, left on the list." She glanced up at him. "Can't you give me a hint? I haven't the faintest clue."

"Someone who didn't realize the significance of what they heard."

She knit her brow. "Someone who didn't realize they were a witness in the first place? We call that an unwitting-witness, at the CID."

"Such a witness can be very helpful, in both police and news work."

"Aye—but first you have to find them, since they don't realize they're a witness."

"You'll get there," he declared. "I have confidence in you."

Doyle smiled. "You're a good egg too, Mr. Maguire."

"Not everyone would agree, Officer Doyle."

But she insisted, "No—you're a trope, too. You're that hubris-person who's had a hard fall, so that you can repent of your pride and save the day."

The ghost smiled. "Now, there's something that hadn't occurred to me. We'll see if I can pull it off."

She knit her brow. "Pull what off, Mr. Maguire?"

But her words only faded into the darkness, as she awakened from her dream.

CHAPTER 28

They were preparing for their meeting with Mrs. Song—Acton in his office, checking on the latest information about the missing reporter and Doyle at the kitchen table, chit-chatting with Adrian whilst she waited for her husband.

The young man had come by to visit with Miss Cherry—their nanny was his aunt, and he didn't see her as often now that he was attending university. He was also keenly aware that Reynolds would be happy to cook-up eggs and bacon at a moment's notice, and the butler was obligingly manning the skillet.

Doyle asked, "How are you, Adrian? I hear crazy women are throwin' themselves at you."

The young man winced. "Poor Maggie—I feel sorry for her, losing her job like that."

"Well, not too sorry, I hope. We see a lot of crazy women in our line of work, so best steer clear—oftentimes they're very good at manipulatin' nice men like yourself."

"Oh, I know—Callie had her number from the start; she

thought something was a little off when Maggie showed up on her doorstep."

"Did she? Faith, what did she want?"

"She was wondering if Callie wanted a roommate—at least until Maggie got herself settled, and had enough money for her own place."

"Callie sent her off, I'll bet. Our Callie's not an easy mark."

He grinned. "More or less. But I really don't think Maggie meant any harm—she just didn't know anyone in the city, except for me."

"I suppose," Doyle agreed fairly. "And she's an artist; sometimes they're not grounded in reality."

"She's a really good artist, I will say that. But she keeps wanting to draw me, which seems a little weird."

"Oh? Are the two of you datin'?"

"No, I'm too busy to date anyone right now. Instead, she just shows up at university with a sketchbook."

A warning bell went off in Doyle's mind, and she cautioned, "You should tell Acton, Adrian—or I will. This borders on stalkin', and you never know when someone's dangerous." Recalled to what Lizzie Williams had said, she repeated, "Sometimes obsessions like this are mental illness, lookin' for an excuse."

But he only shrugged a shoulder. "She seems harmless, though—not aggressive or anything. She's just—just—"

"Underfoot and annoyin'," Doyle filled-in with a smile.

"Right. But I think her heart's in the right place. She even came with me, when I went over to the hospital to see how you were."

Another warning bell sounded in Doyle's head. "Did she indeed?"

"They wouldn't let us in, though—told us you were in critical care and couldn't receive visitors. Sir Vikili was really unhappy about it—he was shouting at a nurse."

There was a small pause, and—carefully hiding her leap of interest—Doyle said in an off-hand manner, "Hard to imagine Sir Vikili raisin' his voice."

"Right—I was shocked."

"Was Acton there?"

"No—or at least, I didn't see him."

No, she thought; Acton was under arrest and meanwhile, it seems that Sir Vikili was creating a mighty ruckus around Acton's injured wife.

Like a hound to the point, Doyle ventured with a show of casual interest, "What was Sir Vikili shoutin' about, could you hear?"

"He said you had to be moved out of critical care, but the nurse was trying to push him out the door." He shook his head slightly. "It was crazy; he was saying he had a court order, or something."

Doyle was silent, as she digested this very interesting tidbit. So; events were suddenly taking shape, and it appeared that Adrian must be the mystery witness that Maguire was referring to—someone who didn't realize the significance of what they'd heard. Magistrate Kirken had been in a panic, and had issued an arrest warrant that would keep her poor husband temporarily under lock and key whilst Sir Vikili—who had a long history of representing the villains in this artwork-rig—claimed he'd a court order and wanted to move the fair Doyle out of critical care. It was very hard to believe—that Sir Vikili would dare do something so underhanded—but here was an eyewitness, and Adrian would have no reason to make it up.

Reynolds brought over Adrian's second breakfast, and Doyle took the opportunity to raise her gaze to the windows as the young man addressed his meal with gusto. Kirken must have issued the order to take custody of Doyle, hoping to gain some leverage over Acton—and what better leverage than to seize the man's wife and then negotiate, somehow?

But—considering this theory—Doyle frowned, slightly. It seemed such a fond hope; it was unclear what Kirken could hope to achieve—and it was doubly-clear that his fate would be sealed, no matter how fond his hopes of holding the fair Doyle hostage. But mayhap the man wasn't thinking clearly—Acton said Kirken wasn't steady, and meanwhile his cohorts were dropping like flies; mayhap this idea was the best the desperate man could come up with. Then, when Officer Shandera allowed Acton to escape and storm the hospital, all desperate plans were abandoned and Kirken had no choice but to flee the scene.

So, this would explain what Adrian had witnessed; the crooked magistrate was trying to lay hands on the fair Doyle—with an assist from Sir Vikili—but Williams wasn't having it, and a brawl ensued. And the next thing you know, Doyle is locked away at Trestles—where court orders mean less than nothing to the people who'd defend the House of Acton to the last yard.

Faith, she thought; I suppose it's a plausible chain of events —who knew, that there was so much goin' on whilst I was out-for-the-count? But there's one major flaw to this working-theory and it's this: why wouldn't Acton just tell me, if this was what happened? There would be no reason to keep it such a closely-guarded secret—especially since the magistrate's fled, and flight is a sure sign of guilt. So, why are all these events shrouded in such secrecy? Faith, it's such a secret that even the hospital staff doesn't know.

Suddenly, she stilled. That wasn't exactly true; it wasn't a secret to Colleen Cadigan—she must have been the nurse who was trying to push Sir Vikili out the door. Cadigan knew what happened, but she hadn't told anyone else despite being the lead nurse and having to physically fight to save her patient. Instead, she'd gone to a mystery-meeting in a park—when? a few days later?—and disappeared.

Although—although she'd clearly told Song about the ruckus, since Song had dropped a few hints to Rachel Anderson about it. But nonetheless, Song had stayed mostly mum about it, too—even though he was a reporter and this was a sensational story. And now the both of them were dead—presumably, anyways—which only seemed to affirm Maguire's strange comment that Acton was the only one who truly knew what had happened.

She frowned, thinking about this. So; it seemed there was a cover-up afoot, orchestrated by none other than her wedded husband—who was the undisputed champion when it came to covering-up things that he didn't want exposed to the light of day. But why was there a need? She could think of no blessed reason to keep any of this a secret—you'd think he'd want just the opposite, in fact. The public would be outraged if they heard about his fake arrest warrant—not to mention the attempt to seize the fair Doyle—and it would only be more burning coals to be heaped atop Magistrate Kirken's head.

Mayhap it was all *too* sensational, and Acton wanted to keep it out of the press? After all, the fact that Sir Vikili had done such a dastardly thing could very well ruin the man's career, if word got out.

But on second thought, that idea didn't hold water. When it came to Acton's wedded wife, all bets were off; her husband wouldn't hesitate to ruin Sir Vikili's career—faith, it was surprising that he hadn't exacted a nasty revenge on Sir Vikili already.

She stilled again. Oh, she realized; unlikely that Acton's planning a nasty revenge if he's suggesting Javid—of all people—as a potential nanny.

Completely bewildered, she conceded that none of this made a thimbleful of sense and so she retreated back to the only thing that seemed to be a certainty, which was that Acton wanted to cover-up the strange and unfathomable events at the hospital. For that matter, so did Song and Cadigan—or at least, they'd kept quiet about it for the days between the donnybrook and their mutual disappearance.

Of course, it was during that same time-frame that Kirken had disappeared—mayhap the two lovers were aligned with Kirken, somehow? Mayhap the crooked magistrate had bribed them to help seize Doyle, so as to allow him to escape? But that theory didn't make much sense, either; if that were the case, then Cadigan wouldn't be fighting with Sir Vikili—instead they would have been allies.

There's a piece to this puzzle I'm missing, she thought for the thousandth time, and reluctantly decided it would be best to change the subject, since Acton was due at any moment.

With a smile at Adrian—who was being handed a second helping by Reynolds—she offered, "Just think; our Miss Cherry is soon to be Mrs. Cherry."

Adrian paused to grin. "I'm really happy for her—my mum, too. She's trying to convince them to come live in Meryton."

"Is she? Faith, it's just our luck to lose yet another nanny."

"Callie would help out," he offered between bites. "She loves your boys."

"Callie's got her own life to manage, my friend. I should have her over, now that everything's back to normal; Acton barred the door to everyone when we were at Trestles, so I haven't seen her in a while."

Adrian paused as though reminded. "My mum was asking me if I knew anything about the man who's being held at Trestles. There's some rumor going around."

This was a surprise, since the man in question had been kept under lock and key for several years now, with no one the wiser. Weighing what to say, Doyle decided it would be no harm to reveal, "There's a mad deacon, livin' in one of the outbuildings—which sounds like a trope if I've ever heard one—but he's harmless. He's an old friend, but since he's a bit mad he's been tucked away for his own good. I'd ask that you say nothin' about him."

Which reminded her that here was another one, who was golden; the mad deacon had helped the fair Doyle in her time of need, and so he's living out the remainder of his years at peaceful Trestles rather than inside a sanitarium for the criminally insane.

Adrian nodded. "All right—mum's the word. He's Irish, I gather?"

"No—it's Grady the stableman who's Irish. This one's a Scotsman."

"You all sound the same to me," he joked.

She laughed. "Cheek—here's Acton; I'll be off."

CHAPTER 29

This interview would take some careful handling. He must never underestimate how clever she was.

Doyle was in the car with her husband on the way over for their visit with Bradford Song's wife—although she was probably his widow, which reminded Doyle that this meeting was going to be a bit tricky.

She asked, "Any updates on the case? Can we tell the woman anythin' encouragin'?"

"I'm afraid not."

Thoughtfully, Doyle regarded him. "You're stewin' like a barleycorn, husband. D'you think she's involved in his murder?"

Slowly, Acton replied, "I am not certain what she knows or doesn't know, and so I'd ask that you make certain to signal, if she is being untruthful on any subject."

This was the standard operating procedure between them; Doyle would brush her hair from her forehead if the witness was lying, and Acton would adjust the interrogation accordingly. The fact that he'd felt it necessary to remind her was of interest, in that it pointed toward the conclusion that he felt Song's wife was indeed involved in the man's murder—she'd have little reason to lie, if she were an innocent and anxious wife.

"Right," she said. "Although I'm not sure that even you can pull this off, Michael—beggin' her for money and accusin' her of murder all in the same sit-down."

"It will be an interesting conversation."

Doyle gazed out the windscreen and frowned, thinking about this next witness on Maguire's list. Rachel Anderson had mentioned that Mrs. Song was undergoing treatment for an undisclosed illness—made it sound as though Song was very concerned about her—and so it seemed a bit strange that the woman would be plotting to murder her husband under those circumstances. Unfortunately, Doyle couldn't mention this to her husband without exposing her discussions with Rachel Anderson and so she'd best button her lip. Hopefully they'd sort it out, soon enough.

"I should mention that we have met Mrs. Song on a previous occasion."

Surprised, Doyle raised her brows. "We have?"

"She is the former Mrs. Sebastian Moran."

Agog, Doyle stared at him. They'd uncovered a very nasty sex trafficking-blackmail rig a few years back—one that involved more than a few judicial officers, along with high-ranking prosecutors—and one of the participants was a respected barrister named Sebastian Moran. During the course of the investigation, they'd interviewed the man's ex-wife and had been left with the conclusion that she'd known all about her husband's participation in the rig, but had turned a blind eye.

"Faith, Michael, here's irony; she's landed in the same pickle as with her first husband—another chouser, involved in questionable doings whilst she's lookin' the other way."

"Wealthy women are often targeted by manipulators."

Doyle nodded. "Aye—cream-pot love, my mum used to say. So; she's the one with the money?"

"Yes. It was what helped her first husband gain his position in such a prestigious Inn of Court."

Thinking back on the previous interview, Doyle remembered, "She struck me as cold to the core—not the sort to be a misguided heroine, fallin' madly in love with the wrong man."

"No, I would agree with that assessment."

She glanced over at him. "Which is why we're doin' a bit of probin', I gather. She may have decided that she doesn't want to go through another divorce but she wants him gone, nonetheless."

"Perhaps," he agreed.

Thinking about this, however, Doyle shook her head slightly. "I didn't get the sense she's the type to be a murderess, Michael. She's instead the type who avoids thinkin' about anything that might distress her."

"We shall see what she has to say."

In due course, they came to the residence—a posh townhouse in West Brompton—and the door was opened immediately by a middle-aged housekeeper. "Good morning, Lord and Lady Acton—Mrs. Song is expecting you; if you will follow me?"

"And you are?" Acton asked politely.

"Oh—I'm Mrs. Radley."

"Does anyone else live on the premises?"

Well, that's interesting, Doyle thought; apparently, we're

wearing our detective-hats straight off the mark. Which is just as well; very hard to imagine Acton's begging for money.

"No; Mrs. Jones—the cook—comes in."

Acton nodded, and then they were ushered into the drawing room where Mrs. Song—who was indeed the former Mrs. Moran—was reclining in an overstuffed chair with an ottoman, a Norwich shawl thrown across her legs.

"Lord and Lady Acton; forgive me for not rising, I have been unwell."

This was apparent to Doyle; the formerly-robust woman was now thin and rather pale, and Doyle was uncomfortably reminded of how her mother had looked when she'd begun sickening.

"Shall we come back at a more convenient time?" Acton asked in sympathy, as he took the woman's hand.

"No, no; I'm much better today than yesterday, as a matter of fact."

"You remember my wife, Kathleen?"

"I do," the woman replied with a small smile as she took Doyle's hand. "So good to see the both of you again. I only wish the circumstances weren't so unhappy."

"Indeed," said Acton. "And I will say immediately that we have no new news."

"I fear the worst," the woman sighed. "It is very unusual for Bradford to drop from sight like this. Please sit down, and make yourselves comfortable."

Not cut-up about it a'tall, Doyle decided; she's well-sick of his shenanigans and probably doesn't much care what's happened to him.

After they were seated, Acton leaned forward in what Doyle would characterize as his sympathetic-detective pose. "I know you have already gone over this ground, Mrs. Song, but is there anything you may have remembered since your initial interview? Was your husband planning to meet with anyone—be it business or personal—around the time he disappeared?"

With a suitably grave expression, the witness shook her head. "Not that I know—I wasn't privy to his calendar. He was so busy, it was hard for me to keep abreast of his day-to-day activities."

Acton pressed, "Did he speak of a new story he was pursuing, perhaps?"

Again, the witness shook her head. "Not that I was aware."

Probably because she'd rather not know what the man was up to, thought Doyle; she was turning a blind eye to his many misdeeds because she didn't want to be embarrassed into having to do something about it.

"And all his electronics have been taken into custody?" Acton asked.

"Yes—everything that was here, anyway."

Doyle could feel her husband's gaze rest briefly upon her but thus far, the woman had spoken the truth in all respects.

Acton apparently decided it was time to get down to brass tacks. "It is believed he was in contact with a woman who worked at the Metro hospital, although we are unsure as to why he was in contact with her."

But Mrs. Song showed no trace of wifely embarrassment, and instead shook her head slightly. "I haven't a clue, I'm afraid."

Again, this was true, and so Acton moved on to his next question. "I understand he traveled quite a bit. Is there any chance he is outside the country?"

"He was often back and forth—mainly to the Continent—but he would always let me know ahead of time." She paused, and then added with a hint of smug satisfaction, "Bradford always brought back a piece of artwork for me, from whichever exhibit he was reviewing. It was his way of making-up for the fact that he was away so much."

Doyle found this reference a bit confusing, and knit her brow. "Wouldn't that be a conflict of interest, to purchase the same art that he was reviewin' for the *World News*?"

Mrs. Song smiled at Doyle in an indulgent manner. "Oh, it's worse than that, my dear; he'd be given a discount—or even be given a piece for free—if the artist could be assured of a glowing write-up."

"Oh," said Doyle, who decided she'd best let her husband handle the questions, henceforth.

Acton continued, "I understand he'd been commissioned to oversee the art gallery in the new marina development; a shame, that the fire destroyed so much of it."

The woman nodded sadly. "Yes—a terrible thing. I suppose it was insured, but money is little compensation for unique works of art."

The penny dropped, and Doyle suddenly realized why Acton had consented to this meeting—Song must have been involved in the artwork money-laundering scheme. Faith, it only made sense, and it should have occurred to her long before now; enlisting a famous art critic would add credibility to the scheme—especially when it came to falsely inflating the prices.

So; it seemed that the Chief Inspector wanted to probe how much the man's wife knew about her husband's involvement—mayhap she could provide new information so as to put the criminal case back on track. Unfortunately, it was apparent she didn't know much—probably by her own choice—and so this little excursion hadn't turned out to be helpful. On the bright side, it now seemed clear that Song's disappearance was directly connected to his involvement in the rig—his was a preemption-murder, plain as day.

They were interrupted when the housekeeper tapped politely on the door jamb. "I've a tea-tray, ma'am."

"Thank you, Radley—and here's my tonic." With a gleam, she lifted an aperitif glass from the tray—one that contained a dark, viscous liquid. "*Crème de cassis*, from the south of France. There's nothing close to this quality here, and so I ask Bradford to fetch me back a case, every year."

As the housekeeper poured their tea, Mrs. Song lifted the crystal glass and unbidden, Doyle suddenly had a memory of another woman, sitting in the Trestles foyer and drinking what seemed to be an innocuous drink.

Leaping to her feet, she deftly intercepted the glass before the woman could take a sip. "I'll take this," she said. And then, turning to Acton, "We should do a tox-screen."

There was a moment of silence, whilst Mrs. Song stared at her in astonishment. "Very well," said Acton. "I will make the appropriate calls."

CHAPTER 30

An interesting twist, to this tale.

Doyle and Acton were standing in the townhouse's entry hall, having a low-voiced conversation as they waited for the detective team Acton had called-in. "She's bein' poisoned, Michael—I'm almost certain of it. You can see that she's not well."

He considered this. "Song's doing, do you think?"

"I imagine. It's a clever delivery-system, since it's sealed bottles of liqueur and he's not here to give it to her. And it all follows—Cadigan was tellin' the other nurses that Song was going to marry her soon, and she'd be rich and famous."

There was a sudden silence, whilst Acton's gaze rested upon hers.

Oh-oh, she thought; time to confess and take my lumps. "I went to visit the nurses—to thank them and take some flowers, Michael. It felt strange that I'd never even met them."

Contrite, he reached to touch her hand. "Yet, you didn't wish me to know."

"No. I know you don't like to talk about it, and so I thought I'd go make a quick visit. I'm sorry I didn't tell you."

"No—it is I who am sorry."

She smiled at him, happy to have got over that rough ground so lightly. "Well, we can both be as sorry as we want, but it's turned out for the best since here we are, solvin' crimes like a house afire. Well—save for Song's disappearance but I gather that you think his was a preemption-murder."

"Yes," he agreed. "He had very questionable ethics."

She made a face. "It doesn't surprise me a'tall—there were some very nasty people involved in that artwork-rig. If Song's the type to try to weasel-out and cast blame elsewhere, small wonder the others decided he was a liability."

"Very sound reasoning," he agreed.

But he said it absently, and she could see that he was distracted. She ventured, "D'you have a guess as to who actually killed him? Elliott and Denisovich were already dead, so it wasn't them. If we can discover who the perps were, mayhap a criminal case can be brought for the murder, since the money-launderin' case has collapsed."

"An excellent notion," he replied.

She went silent, because he was watching his words again and carefully guarding what he told her—same as had been the case with the hospital brawl, and with Sir Vikili's treachery. But —again—it all made little sense; she could think of no blessed reason that he would withhold the fact that Song was involved in the artwork-rig, and had then been murdered for his sins. But nonetheless he'd done so, which only seemed to confirm her strong suspicion that her husband was hip-deep in running some sort of cover-up at the same time he was running a frame-up, so as to bring murder charges against the crooked magistrate. But who was he covering-up for? The true killer? And why would that be?

And as the icing on the cake, he was also orchestrating events so as to pit the villains against each other, so that they'd start eating their own and thereby save the CID the time and trouble of bringing them to justice. Faith, but it must be exhausting to keep track of it all, and her hat was off to him, even as she didn't necessarily approve of all the conniving.

So; it was all very complicated, and small wonder that Williams was issuing warnings to leave things be—even though it hadn't been much of a warning, since the man apparently couldn't bring himself to specify whatever-it-was that he was warning her about—

Holy Mother. Carefully, she lowered her gaze to the fancy rug whilst she entertained a truly gob-smacking notion; if Acton was conducting a cover-up operation even as he was framing-up Kirken for the first two murders, then it was entirely possible— Mother a' Mercy, but it was entirely possible that Acton himself was the one who'd killed Bradford Song, just as he'd killed the first two.

That would certainly explain why he was watching his words so carefully, and hiding things that didn't need to be hidden. After all, if Song was involved in the artwork-rig then Acton would feel he was more than justified in taking a bloody revenge against the man—same as anyone who'd contributed to his wife's ordeal.

She considered this alarming thought, knowing—in the way that she knew things—that she was on to something. Doyle's wedded husband must have decided that justice was taking too winding a road—what with fleeing magistrates and evidence being destroyed—and so he'd just up and killed the wretched man, same as he'd killed Denisovich and Elliott. It would certainly explain why he was trying so hard to keep her in the dark, and it would also explain why he seemed to be in no hurry to return to work—he was busy. Busy doing his vengeance-thing, and orchestrating cover-ups.

And—come to think of it—it would also explain the questions he was putting to Song's wife—about the personnel on premises, and whether all electronics had been secured; he was making certain that his tracks were well-and-truly covered. Acton was the grand master at covering his tracks.

With a knit brow, she continued to contemplate the floor. It was a decent theory, save that there was one obvious flaw; if Acton killed Song, wouldn't that mean he'd killed Cadigan, too? It seemed so hard to believe—the nurse had fought to keep Doyle safe, and—presumably—she'd nothing to do with the artwork-rig. But if Acton hadn't killed Cadigan, why then, had she disappeared?

Her thoughts were interrupted when Officer Gabriel knocked at the door—along with a forensics team—and Acton proceeded to brief them.

Doyle listened to his instructions and thought—interesting; he's called-in Officer Gabriel instead of Williams, which means that whatever he's covering up, Mrs. Song's attempted murder is not a part of it. Instead, this must be the coincidence that Maguire spoke of—he'd said it was a coincidence until it wasn't. So; she'd one-half of the coincidence—they'd stumbled across a murder-plot, separate and apart from the dire events surrounding the marina-fire. And the other half of the coincidence—presumably—was Acton's murder of Song. Song's murder, which had—ironically—saved his wife's life.

CHAPTER 31

He may have to tell her some of it. He could see that she was piecing it together.

They were in the car heading home, and Doyle was hoping that she needn't go over the same rough ground yet again; she'd a feeling her husband had been thrown off his pins by the news about her hospital visit, and that she might be in for a more thorough dressing-down. Well—not a dressing-down, exactly, but a soft sort of scolding wrapped-up in hurt feelings, which was ten times worse. You can fault the Irish for being hot-headed, but there was nothing like a forthright clearing-of-the-air to set things to rights again; the English tended to approach such things sideways, using guile and guilt.

Hoping to avoid her fate, she offered in a bright tone, "A shame we never got a chance to steer some money toward the bakery. On the upside, though, she'll be mighty grateful to us and easily persuaded to unlock the vault."

But her husband wasn't to be distracted from his soft scolding. "I feel badly you were reluctant to tell me of your hospital visit, Kathleen. In the future, perhaps you could keep me advised—you should not have to go to such lengths."

This seemed a reference to the fact she'd managed to ditch Trenton yet again, and it made him uneasy that she was able to do so—which was only fair; he was worried about her, and she shouldn't add to his worries.

"I'm sorry, Michael; I just wanted to go over to thank them and I knew it was a bad memory for you—you'd just as soon bury it deep. It's an odd sort of situation; it was traumatic for you but not for me, since I don't remember it."

"I am not so fragile, perhaps."

This, said with a hint of rebuke—which was only to be expected—and she soothed, "I just wanted to spare you, Michael."

Because—despite his denial and all appearances to the contrary—he was indeed fragile. It was what had drawn her to him from the first, and what made her so fiercely protective of him; beneath all that competent brilliance he'd a troubled mind.

"It is more important that you be honest than you spare my feelings, Kathleen."

She decided that he wasn't the only one who could turn the tables, and so she countered, "It seems to me, husband, that you're not followin' your own advice. You're workin' very hard to keep me in the dark—and as an excellent case-in-point, you didn't think to mention that our Mr. Song was involved in the artwork-rig."

There was a small silence. "I will admit that I am not always able to be honest with you."

She had to smile. "Well, there's an honest statement, at least."

He offered, "I am more honest with you than with anyone."

"Right—and I appreciate it, believe me. Tell me who blacked your eye."

He paused for a moment, thinking this over, and then revealed, "Officer Shandera."

Doyle stared at him in astonishment. "*Shandera* knocked you one? Oh—" she immediately realized; "You let him do it, so that he wouldn't get into trouble for lettin' you escape."

"Yes. He was under orders to detain me, after all."

Shaking her head in wonder, Doyle observed, "Faith, the man will have braggin' rights at *The Bowman* till the crack o' doom."

But her husband cautioned, "Please don't mention it, if you would. I needed to get to the hospital with all speed, and he was willing to allow it."

She slid her gaze his way. "I understand there was a court order, involved." May as well press him, since he seemed to be in the mood to lift the veil a bit.

He admitted, "There was, in a manner of speaking. It was a false order, concocted by Vikili to prevent Magistrate Kirken from attempting to take you into protective custody."

She stared at him, astonished all over again. "*Sir Vikili* faked a court order?"

"Yes. Kirken had asked him to go over to the hospital and present an order placing you in protective custody. Vikili was aware that such a thing was not intended for your benefit, and so he changed the order so as to allow your immediate removal, and informed me of these events."

"Holy *Mother*," she breathed. "And Williams didn't realize that Sir Vikili was on the side of the angels—being as the man's usually on the side of the villains—and so he scrapped with him when he tried to enforce his order."

There was a small pause. "You are remarkably well-informed, Kathleen."

Oh—she'd forgot that she wasn't supposed to know about the donnybrook, and so she immediately decided that the best defense was to go on offense.

Crossly, she retorted, "*Now* I'm well-informed but it's been like pullin' teeth, Michael. A lot of things weren't addin' up, and I wanted to find out what happened—it happened to me, after all."

As expected, this reminder inspired another bout of contrition, and he grasped her hand. "Forgive me, Kathleen. It was a very trying time, and perhaps I haven't handled the aftermath as well as I could have."

She lifted his hand to kiss its back, happy to have got over more rough ground so lightly. "Aye—you were thinkin' 'least said, soonest mended' but you'd forgot who you were dealin' with, here."

"Indeed," he agreed with the ghost of a smile.

To cheer him up—the memory of these events did seem to make him rather grim—she teased, "Hard to believe Sir Vikili could lay a glove on Williams."

"Vikili enlisted Savoie to accompany him to the hospital, and between them they persuaded Williams to rethink his actions."

"Oh—good on Sir Vikili, to realize he'd best bring along some muscle."

"Yes."

She paused to consider these events with all the wonder they deserved. "Faith; it's lucky, you are, that you've a rasher of staunch supporters."

The faint smile appeared again. "As do you; I might mention that Reynolds took it upon himself to bring a handgun to the hospital, since he was unable to contact Trenton and feared the worst."

"*No*," she breathed, astonished yet again.

"Upon his arrival, he came upon the—misunderstanding—between the others, and convinced everyone to stand down. I arrived shortly thereafter."

She couldn't help but laugh at the imagined scene. "You must have thought you'd stumbled into upside-down world."

"I enforced Vikili's false order and you were immediately transported to Trestles."

Slowly, she shook her head. "Mother a' Mercy, but there's a tale."

His chest rose and fell. "I wished to spare you much of it."

She glanced his way. "It seems that the crooked magistrate has a lot to answer for—he's the ultimate villain, in this tale. Strange, that we've still not hide nor hair of him."

"I have every confidence he will resurface."

This was true, and something of a surprise; Doyle had begun to entertain the shrewd notion that the magistrate had met the same fate as the others; if her theory was correct—that he was slated to take the fall for all the other murders—than there was no need for her vengeful husband to keep the man alive so as to refute whatever evidence Williams was cooking-up against him.

But Acton's words were true, and so it seemed that the man was indeed alive, and on the lam. Thinking about this, she admitted, "I'm half-relieved they can't find him, Michael; he's the only player left—at least for the London aspect of the artwork-rig—and until they find him I'll not have to testify. It makes me feel a bit guilty but it's true; I wasn't lookin' forward to havin' to go over it all again, and then havin' to face down Sir Vikili on the cross-exam."

"A silver lining, then."

"Along with Mrs. Song—savin' the rich lady in the nick o' time."

"Good catch," he said, and squeezed her hand.

CHAPTER 32

That night, Doyle rather reluctantly confessed to Maguire, "The more I think about it, the more I think he's left out some important parts of this tale."

The ghost bowed his head in acknowledgement. "He's very good at thinking on his feet, and parsing information to serve his ends."

She made a wry mouth. "No one knows this better than me, my friend. And it's odd that he didn't mention Cadigan, even though Adrian said she was in the thick of the dust-up. Mainly it's odd because I was already wonderin' if Acton's killed her—I'm almost certain he's killed Song. But why is Cadigan dead? She's wasn't involved in the rig—or at least, there's no hint of such. Instead, she obviously meant well, when she was barrin' the door to Sir Vikili and fightin' to keep me at the hospital."

"Cadigan is an Irish name."

Doyle blinked at him. "She was murdered because she was Irish? Acton may be mad, Mr. Maguire, but he's not *that* mad."

Since he didn't respond, she continued to muse aloud, "And

I was that surprised to hear that Kirken isn't dead, yet. Acton says the CID doesn't know where he is, but I find it very hard to believe that *he* doesn't know—Acton's a wizard, at trackin' people down. And he'd definitely want the man dead, if the plan is to frame Kirken for all the other murders—nothin' more annoyin' than having your frame-up victim still alive, to refute all your manufactured evidence."

"A very good point."

"Aye." She grimaced, thinking about it. "Acton wouldn't have a shred of mercy for the man, but he's not been drawn-and-quartered—not yet, leastways, because Acton said he thinks Kirken will resurface soon, and it was true."

She frowned, thinking about this. "I suppose it's possible that Acton truly doesn't know where Kirken is hidin' out."

Maguire gave her a dubious look.

"Hard to believe," she acknowledged. "But on the other hand, if Acton knew how to find Kirken, you'd think the man would already be dead—and not in a nice way."

"So, you would think," Maguire agreed.

Suddenly struck, Doyle stared at him. "Oh—the trap is for Kirken? That's what Acton's about?"

"Very good," her ghostly companion said with approval.

Frowning, Doyle considered this revelation, and then slowly shook her head. "I don't know, Mr. Maguire. All things considered, Acton's miles more likely to murder the man rather than set-up a trap to bring him in, all peaceful-like. Acton's got murder-in-the-blood—especially when it comes to vengeance."

"As we have seen," Maguire agreed.

Reminded, she added, "And there's another thing, too—he knows I'd hate to have to testify in the criminal case, but if Kirken's brought-in alive, the trial will be back on-track."

"A very good point."

Utterly perplexed, Doyle asked, "So; why isn't Kirken dead? And—on the other hand—why is Cadigan? You'd think it would be the opposite. Who did Cadigan meet, when she went to the park that night? Acton? She wouldn't go to meet Acton on the quiet, I think—especially after the brouhaha at the hospital. More likely she went to meet Song—"

She lifted her head. "Oh. If Acton killed Song—which I think he did—he'd have the man's mobile. Acton must have lured her in, usin' Song's phone."

"Very impressive," said Maguire.

But Doyle shook her head slowly. "I don't know *why*, though; from all accounts she was tryin' to protect me, and Acton would be grateful for that—instead of plottin' to kill her. Although mayhap she's another one involved in the artwork-rig—mayhap she was helpin' Song, in some way."

The ghost offered, "Don't forget there's another witness."

In some surprise, she stared at him. "But I thought the mystery-witness was Adrian—he caught a glimpse of the donnybrook, and saw Cadigan wrestlin' with Sir Vikili."

"A good lead," the ghost agreed. "But it's not him."

"Trenton?" she guessed. "Where was Trenton anyways, durin' this whole holy-show? He's unaccounted-for; Reynolds couldn't raise him but Acton's never said where the man was. And I don't get the sense that Acton is unhappy with Trenton, for not bein' available when he was needed most."

"Trenton was carrying out a commission."

Bewildered, she stared at him. "That makes no sense, though; nothin' would have been more important for Trenton than protectin' me at the hospital—doubly so, if Acton's been arrested on a trumped-up charge. So; what sort of commission could have possibly pulled Trenton away? I don't dare ask the man—he'd be more buttoned-up than Williams and he'd grass me out to Acton in a heartbeat."

"Yes. All very interesting, isn't it?"

"Aye," she nodded slowly. "That's the part of the story that Acton's parsin', isn't it?"

"You must find out—it's important."

"But, how can I?" she reasoned. "The only people who know aren't goin' to tell me, for love or money."

But once again, the question went unanswered as she stared into the darkness of her room.

CHAPTER 33

He was more than ready for the denouement. Unfortunate, that it was necessary.

The following morning, they were walking to drop-off Edward at school when Acton's mobile pinged and he handed the push-chair over the Doyle to take the call. "Lizzie Williams," he explained. "With preliminary results."

He listened for a few moments without comment, and then said, "Thank you."

He rang off and said, "You were right."

"Poison," Doyle pronounced, unsurprised.

"Yes. The markers show the sample contained an excess dose of digoxin."

Since Tommy was loudly insisting, Doyle relinquished the push-car back to her husband. "Which is?"

"It's a type of heart medication that has a narrow application, at present. It dissipates quickly in the body, and so it would be difficult to detect in an autopsy." He glanced at her. "And I imagine even if it were discovered, Song would argue that it was a mercy-killing, due to his wife's supposed illness."

"Holy *Mother*," she breathed. "That's why he was on the bandwagon—just in case he needed the defense, himself."

"As a celebrity, he may have very well been believed."

"Aye; the public's not near as cynical as they should be." She shook her head. "Song was cold to the core, it seems."

"He's not the only one; because the drug's use is fairly limited, it was most likely stolen from the hospital by someone who had access."

She blew out a dismayed breath. "So; it seems that Cadigan's not a misguided heroine after all—she's an out-and-out villainess."

"Yes. She was obviously complicit, if she was boasting that she'd soon marry Song."

Eying him sidelong, she ventured," A shame, that we can't put a pin on her whereabouts so as to slap some cuffs on the woman."

"I will have Officer Gabriel put out an All Ports Warning," he replied, mild as milk.

Exasperating man, Doyle thought as she turned her attention back to the pathway ahead. And I've still no idea why he's presumably murdered the wretched woman; he didn't know a blessed thing about her involvement in Mrs. Song's murder plot—he didn't even know there was a murder plot to begin with—I'm sure of it.

After deciding she may as well take the bull by the horns, she remarked, "I've the strong feelin', husband, that you know more about what's happened to Nurse Cadigan than you pretend."

"Perhaps," he agreed in the same mild tone. "But it hardly matters, anymore."

Very true, thought Doyle in grudging acknowledgement; because—in Maguire's words—it was a coincidence, until it wasn't. Acton took it upon himself to kill Cadigan for reasons unknown and—ironically—by doing so he interrupted a murder-plot.

Which—come to think of it—was half the reason for his vigilantism. He shouldn't be murdering villains outside the justice system, of course, but one could assume that by doing so he was saving unknown lives—those innocent people who would have suffered had the villain been allowed to continue on. And the other half of the reason, of course, was sheer bloody-minded vengeance.

For Acton, either one was justification enough—but it was a very dangerous sort of power, to decide that you should act as judge and jury; the whole purpose of the justice system was to protect ordinary folk from powerful and dangerous people. All very ironic, it was.

"Tim will come over for your check-up early this afternoon, if you are willing."

Eagerly, she looked over at him. "And he's goin' to clear me for work, right?"

"If he considers you fit."

"Faith—I'm fit as a fiddle," she declared. "Look at me, solvin' crimes, left and right."

"I will be cleared today also, I imagine. My hearing will go forward this afternoon, but I expect it will take some time. Don't expect me to return before the boys go to bed."

Doyle blew out a breath of relief. "Thank all the blessed saints and angels—you're not cut out to be a house-husband."

"On the contrary, I have very much enjoyed this time together."

This was true, and she reached to pull him against her side in a half-hug, as he pushed Tommy's push-chair. "Nothin' like havin' a close call, to make you appreciate the ordinary things."

"Yes," he agreed in a quiet tone.

Mentally she winced a bit, because the reminder had saddened him—she shouldn't have spoken so lightly, since he wasn't a "lightly" sort of person. In gentle remonstrance, she said, "Promise me, Michael, that you won't mope about if I'm gathered-up early instead of late. You'll have to carry on, and marry some nice woman who'll love the boyos."

"I will never marry again," he said, and it was true.

She decided not to pursue the topic—she truly needed to think before she gabbled-off whatever was on her mind—and so instead she said, "Well then; you and Tim can manage it between you—two old bachelors, handling the three-ring circus."

"McGonigal does have access to sedatives," he noted.

CHAPTER 34

That afternoon, after Acton had left for his meeting with Professional Standards, Doyle opened the door to Tim McGonigal.

McGonigal stood as Acton's oldest friend from university days—his only friend, truly—and even at that, the two men weren't exactly close. He was a genial, kind man—and it rather boggled the mind to think that the two were compatible—but nevertheless, Tim was another staunch supporter who'd helped see them through some of their more harrowing adventures.

Unfortunately, McGonigal did seem slated to remain a bachelor since he tended to fall for women who hadn't fallen for him. It was a shame—the man was a successful doctor, and back in Ireland the local *basadóir* would have had him buckled-up with no further ado.

"How are you, Tim?" Doyle asked, as they descended the stairway down toward the master suite.

"I'm just fine; more importantly, how are you, Kathleen? Gave us all quite a scare."

"You're well-used to it by now, Tim; it's old hat."

He chuckled, and—curious as to how much he knew about the events on that disaster-day—she asked, "When were you called-in, like the cavalry? I know Acton wasn't very happy with the personnel at the hospital."

"That's true," he agreed, and didn't offer anything further, being as he was loyal to his friend and wasn't even going to give the man's equally-loyal wife chapter-and-verse about the aforesaid bad behavior.

Changing tack, Doyle offered, "Trestles was the perfect place to recover, though— all that peacefulness, and such. Although poor Grady was put through his paces, what with Acton's clearin' everyone out."

They'd come to the bedroom, and Doyle seated herself on the edge of the bed whilst McGonigal opened up his medical kit. "Yes; it was a bit strange with the place so silent. Made you think there were ghosts around every corner."

"Aye, that," Doyle agreed.

"But it served the purpose." He lowered his voice. "Acton had to keep it all very mum. The witness, you know—the young Irishman."

Doyle blinked. "Seamus Riordan?"

"Oh." Her companion gave a quick glance her way. "Perhaps I shouldn't have said."

Retrenching, Doyle assured him, "Oh no; I knew Acton had him tucked-away—he's a prime witness and very much at-risk. I just didn't realize he was tucked-away at Trestles. I suppose it comes in very handy, to have a castle keep."

McGonigal indicated she should roll up her sleeve. "A nice young man—I examined him, since he'd been banged up a bit. Nothing serious, thankfully."

Doyle watched him as he fixed the blood pressure cuff on her arm. "Aye—I think he's the one that fished me out of the water."

McGonigal raised his brows. "Did he? Good on him—I must say that he doesn't seem the heroic type. And yet he's willing to be a whistleblower and put himself at risk. You always wonder whether you'd do the same, if you were in his position."

As he removed the cuff, Doyle could only agree. "Aye, that; there are some nasty people involved in that rig." Or at least there were, she mentally corrected; lately, there's mainly smoldering ruins as far as the eye can see.

"If you would hold your head still, and have your eyes follow my finger."

As she complied, she thought over the interesting fact that Seamus Riordan was tucked away at Trestles—the same place she'd been tucked away—but she hadn't been informed of it. Of course, as McGonigal had pointed out, it was all very hush-hush and she did tend to say the wrong thing to the wrong person. But obviously, it wasn't as hush-hush as they'd like—McGonigal knew of it, and so had Adrian—he'd said there was a rumor going around Meryton about an Irishman being held at Trestles.

"If you would stand on one leg, Kathleen; and then the other."

As Doyle complied, the doctor asked a few memory-questions, and then had her sit again so that he could shine a little torch into each eye. He then tapped her knees with a hammer to test her reflexes.

"Everything looks good," the doctor pronounced as he straightened up. "No signs of damage—the hospital did the right thing by putting you into an induced-coma protocol; you can never be too careful when it comes to a brain injury."

He smiled slightly, as he turned to put his hammer away.

"You were speaking, though—in delirium, which is often the case when the brain has swelled and put pressure on the stem."

Doyle nodded, remembering what the nurses had said. "Reticulator-somethin'."

"Yes—very good." He paused to chuckle at the memory. "It was somewhat alarming, actually; you told me you'd been speaking with my mother, even though she passed away many years ago."

He bent to rummage in his medical bag as Doyle stared at him, horrified.

After retrieving a fetal listening monitor, he turned to face her and indicated she should lay back. "I only wish it could have been true; I miss her still."

As she lay back on the bed, Doyle managed to say through stiff lips, "I hope I didn't say anythin' embarrassin', Tim."

"Oh, no—not at all. I'm going to unbutton your shirt so we can listen to the baby." As he did so, he gave her a teasing look. "I've strict instructions to draw no blood, though—no needles, I promise."

He proceeded to smear a lubricant on her abdomen whilst she gripped the bed-covers in her hands and tried to control her racing thoughts—but there was nothing for it; her mind would not stay silent.

I'm forever saying the wrong thing to the wrong person, she thought with acute dismay; even when I'm conked-out, apparently. And here was the mystery witness, just as Maguire had said; someone who didn't realize the significance of what he'd heard. Not like Colleen Cadigan, who—apparently—understood the significance very well; after all, Cadigan was Irish. The fair Doyle had been careful to hide her perceptive abilities all her life, but in this one instance it had been out of her hands and she'd exposed herself—all unknowing—to someone who—coincidentally—knew what it was that she was hearing.

And it didn't end there; Cadigan must have told Song—her beau, whose cohorts were dead and who desperately needed leverage to avoid the same fate. Leverage that Colleen Cadigan handed to him on a silver platter.

My working-theory was close, Doyle realized as the faint sound of little Mary's heartbeat filled the room—but I didn't have it quite right; Song's was indeed a preemption-murder but not for the reasons I suspected. Instead, the man must have contacted Acton, threatening to reveal my secret unless his own role in the rig was kept quiet. And Acton, true to form, had immediately solved the problem without batting an eye.

As Maguire would put it, he'd squashed Song like an annoying insect and then he'd lured-in Cadigan for the same fate. No one could know his wife's secret, and small wonder that Williams was spooked—Williams, who was no doubt enlisted in all this as a not-so-subtle warning.

With dawning realization, she was reminded of the careful questions Acton had asked Song's wife, and how he wanted to know every person who may have come into contact with Song in his home—right down to the cook. If necessary, he would have extinguished every possible loose-end—like the wicks from so many candles; carefully and methodically buttoning it all up so that there would be no one left to leak Doyle's secret.

And so, what Maguire had said was true—no one knew what had happened, save Acton. Even McGonigal didn't know, because McGonigal was a doctor and not one who would think that Doyle's babbling about ghosts was anything other than what could be expected from a brain injury.

Suddenly, she stilled. Hold on, though; she was forgetting someone—Seamus Riordan. Riordan, who was apparently under lock-and-key at Trestles. Why was that, if the case was at a standstill? Mother a' Mercy—did Acton know Riordan was a fellow-traveler, and therefore would know about Doyle's abilities? Possibly—her husband had mentioned that Riordan knew exactly where she'd sunk into the murky Thames and Acton, after all, was very quick on the uptake.

McGonigal unfastened the monitor, and wiped the lubricant from her abdomen with a tissue. "She sounds good, Kathleen. You may button-up, again."

Doyle sat up, and buttoned her shirt with fumbling fingers as she realized—Holy Mother—she realized that if Acton knew that Riordan knew, her husband would have a terrible dilemma. In the usual course of things, Riordan would be another wick to be extinguished but Riordan had saved the fair Doyle's life, and therefore Acton owed the man a debt that he could never repay.

Almost immediately, however, she was reminded that her husband wasn't acting like a man on the horns of a dilemma. Instead, he was acting like he did when he was patiently weaving a web—focused, and determined. Because he was up to something, and it wasn't hard to imagine his aim; even a debt-of-honor would mean nothing when it came to safeguarding his wife—after all, he'd once gone after Savoie even though he owed Savoie the same sort of debt. In Acton-world, his wife took priority, and everything else would be—regrettably, perhaps—sacrificed to protect her.

That was why he hadn't told her about Riordan's being at Trestles, and that was why Trestles was working with a skeleton staff; Seamus Riordan was slated to be another preemption-murder—one more, to be folded into this artwork-case. There'd been a few already; faith, it was no doubt the main reason Acton had killed the other two men immediately—no one would think it strange if the prime witness was also targeted by the same unknown killers, and was thus caught-up in the panicked fall-out.

It also explained Acton's unhappy piano-playing; the man had to steel himself, because his honor would dictate otherwise, but if the choice was between his honor and his wife, his wife would win, every time.

But this rather grim realization didn't explain Acton's plan; if he intended to snuff-out this particular wick, why hadn't he done so immediately?

"All's good," McGonigal pronounced.

Her attention brought back to the matter at hand, Doyle managed to reply, "Aye; Mary's a hardy little thing."

"Like her mother," he joked.

She managed a small smile. "You'd think I'd nine lives, like a cat."

McGonigal sobered a bit. "You were definitely very lucky; a few more minutes underwater and there probably would have been lasting damage—both to you and to the baby."

Oh, thought Doyle, as she stared at him in dismay; it seems I have my very own debt-of-honor. I suppose I've got to go see what's-what, and save Seamus Riordan from whatever fate Acton's got planned for him.

CHAPTER 35

They mounted the stairs back to the main floor, with Doyle turning over possible scenarios in her mind; surprise was her most potent weapon, since Acton didn't know she knew Riordan was at Trestles. And there was no time like the present, with Acton tied-up in the Professional Standards hearing for the remainder of the day. She needed a driver—truly, one of these days she should make a push, and learn to drive—and the driver had to be someone who wouldn't grass her out to Acton in a heartbeat. Williams? Best not; the poor man was spooked.

As Reynolds walked over to open the door for McGonigal, he informed Doyle, "There is a young woman in the lobby, madam, asking if she could speak to you for a moment. A Ms. Rachel Anderson."

"Oh—I'll walk you down, Tim. She's a reporter, and I should hear what she's got to say."

And so, when Doyle emerged from the lift with McGonigal it

was to see Anderson, waiting rather self-consciously by the Concierge desk. The young woman was pale and drawn, and didn't appear to have been sleeping well. "Lady Acton; I was wondering if you could give me a statement. I understand the CID has opened an investigation into the attempted murder of Bradford's—of Mrs. Song."

Poor thing, Doyle thought with a pang of sympathy; she's come to the part of the story where she's starting to realize how misguided she's been. "I'm afraid I can't make a statement, Ms. Anderson. Not without clearance from PR."

The young woman lowered her voice. "Can you tell me anything off-the-record?"

Somberly, Doyle informed her, "It's as bad as it seems, I'm afraid."

The other woman pressed her pale lips together for a moment. "Have they located Mr. Song yet?"

No, and they never will, thought Doyle, but she said only, "I'm not privy, I'm afraid."

There was a small, stricken silence and then McGonigal stepped forward. "Are you all right, miss? I'm a doctor; perhaps you should sit down for a moment—here, here's a bench."

With a visible effort, Anderson pulled herself together and offered-up a wan smile. "No—I'm all right. I should be going."

"Then may I give you a lift? Lady Acton can vouch for me."

Recalled to her manners, Doyle said, "Oh—sorry; Rachel Anderson, this is Tim McGonigal."

"Pleased to meet you," said Rachel. "Sorry about all the drama—I'm a reporter with the *World News*."

"Are you? I'd better watch what I say, then."

Since by all appearances, he was the last person to be involved in anything remotely newsworthy, Anderson's smile became genuine. "Thank you; I'd appreciate a lift."

Thoughtfully, Doyle watched them leave through the revolving door and then she pulled her mobile and rang-up Reynolds. "Could you come down to the lobby, please? I've a favor to ask."

CHAPTER 36

Surreptitiously, Doyle slid her mobile onto the edge of the Concierge desk where she could claim to have forgot it, and when Reynolds appeared, she immediately steered him back into the lift. "I'd like to take a flyin' visit to Trestles, if you don't mind."

The servant was understandably surprised, as she pressed the button that would take them to the parking garage. "Now, madam?"

"Now." Acton's hearing should be just getting started, and so she'd some time before he realized that his mad wife had slipped the leash. "I want to check on somethin' over there, and may as well go now."

Recovering from his surprise, the servant offered, "Shall I have Mr. Trenton accompany us, madam?"

"No need; Trenton's with Cherry and Tommy, and we can manage on our own."

"Very good, madam." There was a small pause. "Is Mr. Hudson aware that you will be paying a visit?"

"We're goin' to surprise him," Doyle informed him, as the doors slid open. "It will be a laugh-and-a-half."

The servant considered this in dismayed silence as they descended into the garage, and then offered, "I'm not certain Mr. Hudson is one who tolerates the unexpected very well, madam."

Doyle smiled. "You'd be surprised, my friend."

"Have we a driver?"

"You're the driver. We'll take the Range Rover."

"I believe Lord Acton has the Range Rover, madam."

"Oh," said Doyle, pausing to contemplate this setback. "I didn't want to use the Concierge limo, so I suppose we can take the train—there's a station in Meryton." She lifted her hand to press the button to ascend to the lobby again.

"We can take my car, madam," the servant offered.

She brightened. "Yes—let's do that."

And so, they drove to Trestles in Reynolds' small sedan, which—as could be expected—was neat and serviceable. It was quite a bit nosier on the open highway than the Range Rover which was a good thing, all in all, in that conversation was limited—not to mention that it had started to rain, which meant the wipers only added to the general noise.

Nevertheless, it wasn't long before the servant decided he needed to assess this rather strange situation. Raising his voice, he asked, "Have we an errand to perform, madam?"

"I'm not sure," she advised, trying to decide how much to tell him, and wishing she was as talented as her husband in parsing words. She decided to admit, "It's one of those things where I've got a hunch, and mayhap Acton wouldn't exactly approve, but it's all for the best."

Reynolds, as could be expected, suppressed a flare of anxiety but replied in a stoic tone, "If you say so, madam."

Good, she thought; he's decided that whatever's afoot, he should button his lip and accompany me so as to offer his aid—it's what Acton would want him to do, after all.

Half-teasing, she asked, "Did you bring your gun?"

She intercepted another flare of alarm. "I did not madam. Do you believe I will need it?"

"I hope not, but Grady's somethin' of a wild-card."

Again, her companion ventured, "Perhaps it would be wise to ring-up Mr. Hudson, madam. Just to inform him that we are *en route*."

She could understand the man's concern, in that the servant-pecking-order put the steward-of-the-ancestral-estate above the London-flat's-butler, and the last needful thing for Reynolds was to cross Hudson, since he was hoping to be the man's successor, someday.

And so, Doyle explained, "No; we'll surprise him. The element of surprise comes in very handy, in police work—it's never a good idea to give the suspects time to assess the situation, or to call-in reinforcements."

Carefully, Reynolds inquired, "Are there suspects at Trestles, madam?"

"Oh, no—I was just speakin' in general terms."

After a moment's consideration, the servant ventured, "Did the reporter in the lobby give you a tip, madam?"

Doyle smiled. "No; believe it or not, I'm the one who's givin' her tips, poor thing. But I think things are turnin' around for her, and I wonder what it was that Tim's mother wanted to say to him."

At sea, Reynolds asked, "Dr. McGonigal is involved, madam?"

"I hope so," she replied. "Cross your fingers."

They drove in silence for a few minutes, and since Reynolds

was all on-end, Doyle decided she should make an attempt to smooth him down a bit. Again, she raised her voice to address him. "I understand you showed-up at the hospital to save the day, Reynolds. A shame we've no more jade axes."

Carefully, the butler replied, "I am afraid I am not at liberty to speak on this subject, madam."

"Right—Acton was tryin' to keep me in the dark, but that's a faint hope and so I pieced it all together and he's the one who told me about your showin' up to knock some heads together. Faith, we're lucky you didn't have to shoot Williams—Lizzie's not the type to take such a thing lyin' down."

The servant unbent enough to disclose, "Mr. Savoie was very helpful in convincing Mr. Williams that he was mistaken in his assessment of the situation."

Aye, Doyle thought; Savoie's the only one who could best Williams, but no doubt the fact that Reynolds seemed to trust Savoie helped to settle Williams down. Not a single one of them would trust Sir Vikili a blessed inch, however, so it's lucky that Acton was set free to put everything to rights.

Thinking about this, Doyle remarked, "Amazin', that Sir Vikili risked so much; he can't betray his clients without sufferin' the consequences—which is why it's not a good idea to represent ruthless blacklegs in the first place. But Sir Vikili owes Acton—he owes Acton many times over—and to people like them, that's miles more important than who represents who."

"Whom," Reynolds offered.

"Thanks—whom."

After a moment's silence, during which the wipers clapped in rhythm, Doyle smiled. "A shame that I missed out on all this, Reynolds—I'll bet Acton was breathin' fire."

"A very unpleasant situation, madam."

Yes, she thought as she turned her gaze out the window to

watch the rain. And then—the next day, mayhap?—Song tried to blackmail Acton, which left the man with yet another crisis; making sure no one was left alive to reveal his Irish bride's strange and unworldly abilities. Save for Seamus Riordan, who must have been taken from the marina-fire straight to Trestles— that was Trenton's commission, the one that took priority over everything else. Riordan would be held at Trestles—mayhap indefinitely, since Acton had to think long and hard about what to do with the young man.

Interesting, that word of his captivity seemed to be leaking out; she'd never heard a blessed whisper about the mad deacon, and he'd been there for years. But the whispers about Riordan would only put more pressure on Acton to extinguish this one last wick, and so she'd best gird her loins and go rescue the wretched man. With any luck, she'd never have to deal with him again.

CHAPTER 37

Trestles' massive front doors were opened by Hudson himself—he was aware they'd arrived, since the gateman had let them through—and the stately servant bowed to her in greeting. "Good afternoon, madam. What a pleasant surprise."

"We're here to bring solace to the prisoner," Doyle informed him.

Hudson asked politely, "Which prisoner is that, madam?"

"Not the deacon; instead the one that's locked-away in the garret."

She'd made an educated guess that this was where they were holding Riordan; it only made sense—the topmost floor was the servant's quarters, and Acton had cleared them all out.

Hudson did not betray by the flicker of an eyelash that such a request was dismaying, even though the poor man was indeed dismayed. "If you would allow me to consult with Lord Acton, madam."

But Doyle shook her head. "No such luck, my friend; Acton's

in the middle of an important hearin' and he can't be reached, just now. Instead you'll just have to trust that I know what I'm doin'."

There was a small silence since this was, after all, quite the ask.

In respectful tones, Reynolds spoke up. "I believe, Mr. Hudson, that we should allow Lady Acton access as she requests."

Hudson made a quarter-turn and addressed his fellow servant with a hint of censure. "I am afraid I have strict instructions, Mr. Reynolds, and my decisions must take precedence, here."

"Quite right, Mr. Hudson. However, I would venture to point out that Lady Acton's wishes must take precedence over our own."

In an even tone, Hudson replied, "But such would not be the case if Lord Acton countermands Lady Acton's wishes, Mr. Reynolds."

"Just so. However—if I may venture to say so, sir—there is little chance of that."

There was a small pause, and then Hudson condescended to bow his head slightly. "You may have the right of it, Mr. Reynolds. Come this way, then."

Hudson then led them through the silent house to the servants' staircase, where they mounted the stairs to the third floor—located under the ancient eaves, where the servants were normally quartered. He then led them down the hallway until he paused before an ancient oaken door. As he raised his hand to knock, however, Doyle noted with some surprise that the door didn't seem to be locked, and so she stayed his arm. I'll take it from here, Hudson."

There was no need to stage her entry as though Riordan was

a perp, because she knew—in the way that she knew things—that the Irishman was as harmless as a kitten. Therefore, she gave a perfunctory rap on the door as she swung it open.

To her surprise, an unexpected tableau met her gaze. Seamus Riordan was standing beside the bed in the well-lit, well-appointed room, in the process of packing his suitcase. He didn't appear constrained in any way, and a tea-tray sat on the desk by the windows, waiting to be cleared.

"Oh," the young man said in surprise. "'Tis you."

"'Tis," she answered. There was a long pause, whilst she contemplated the interesting fact that he didn't seem the least bit anxious or worried. "I've come to check on you," she explained rather lamely. "You're leavin'?"

"I am," he agreed. "I've been cleared to go home—the criminal case has been put on hold."

"Aye," she affirmed, still trying to process this unexpected situation. It certainly seemed that she'd been worried about nothing, and Acton didn't have a dilemma about Rirodan, after all.

She was suddenly struck with a dismaying thought—Holy Mother; could it be that Acton didn't even *know* that Riordan knew about Doyle? Mayhap the Irishman wasn't even on the list, as a wick to be snuffed? Faith, if that were indeed the case, she'd put the cat amongst the pigeons by coming here—how ironic would it be, if she exposed the man to Acton's tender mercies after he'd heroically saved her life? She needed to be fast on her feet, for once, and try to mend the situation as best she could.

Putting on a friendly face, she advised, "I'd a free afternoon and I wanted to drive up to thank you personally. For savin' my life, and all."

The young man smiled. "Happy I was handy, Lady Acton."

To add credibility to her story, she offered, "Would you mind sittin' for another tea, downstairs? I'd love to hear the tale."

For whatever reason, she was immediately aware that he knew she wasn't being sincere, as he bent to zip-up the suitcase. "I'm afraid I've a train to catch, Lady Acton. Next time you're in Dublin, though."

Suddenly ashamed, she said in Gaelic, "I'm sorry. You make me uneasy."

"I know," he replied in the same language. "Not to worry—I understand."

In English, she offered, "Let me drive you to the station, then—it's the least I can do."

"Thank you—that would be much appreciated."

Reynolds moved over to take the man's suitcase, and Doyle admitted, "I'll have to have someone else drive us, actually. I'm not much of a driver, myself."

Hudson offered, "Grady was planning to do the honors, madam. A ternary of Irishmen, if I may say so."

"Just grand," said Doyle, pinning on her brightest smile.

CHAPTER 38

And so, a short time later Doyle found herself seated between Riordan and Grady in the front seat of Grady's truck, as the taciturn gamekeeper drove them over to the train station.

The silence stretched to the point of awkwardness and Doyle thought; I've had plenty of experience watching my husband be polite to people he didn't much care for—you'd think I'd have picked up some pointers over the years.

"At least it's stopped rainin'," she ventured, and congratulated herself on finding a safe topic.

"Aye," Grady agreed.

A small silence ensued. "What's the weather like in Dublin?" Doyle asked Riordan.

"I haven't checked on it," the man replied. "I'll be happy to be home, though."

"You've been very brave—to be willin' to do this," Doyle noted fairly. "Not everyone would have agreed to testify."

"Testify about what?" asked Grady.

Doyle decided it was safe to say, "Mr. Riordan was goin' to testify in a criminal case, but he's not needed anymore."

Grady smiled slightly. "Not against Laddie, I hope."

Riordan also offered a small smile but made no reply, and Doyle joked, "Never say Laddie went after you, too? Faith, the dog must be a Protestant."

But this sally didn't have the desired effect, and Grady sank into a tight-lipped silence. Don't joke about religion, Doyle hurriedly chastised herself; mental note.

Since she felt she couldn't possibly speak about the weather again, she said, "Our Callie's goin' to miss you, Mr. Riordan; I suppose now she'll have to enlist Reynolds to help her with her coursework."

But this remark only caused Riordan to tighten his lips in turn. "I hope she keeps with it."

Rather desperately, Doyle added, "Her mum's comin' back soon. From Paris."

Grady frowned in confusion. "Callie's mum's in town, Lady Acton—I saw her only yesterday."

"Oh—Callie's other mum," Doyle corrected.

Riordan raised his brows. "Callie has two mums?"

"In a manner of speakin'," Doyle said vaguely, and wished rather crossly that she hadn't signed up for this stupid car ride—which was exactly what she deserved for feeling guilty when she'd no reason to feel guilty a'tall; people saved other people's lives *all* the time.

Except that they didn't, of course, and—ashamed all over again—Doyle made a mighty effort to say something to ease the atmosphere. "I'll have you know that Grady makes a mean pasty, Mr. Riordan. It's half the reason we come to Trestles as often as we do."

Riordan seemed willing to soften, and said to Grady, "Now,

there's a talent. Nothing like a hot pasty on a cold day like this one."

Grady smiled slightly. "Along with a glass of beer."

"Depends on the beer," Riordan noted.

"Lager is best with pasties," Grady opined.

"I prefer a brown ale, myself."

"That's fair," Grady acknowledged. "So long as it's not an India."

"Never," Riordan agreed, with a great deal of firmness.

Mental note, thought Doyle as she listened to their discussion with a sense of relief; you can't go wrong if you can get men talking about beer.

The rest of the car ride was spent in a general discussion of football clubs and their relative merits—since this subject was closely-adjacent to the topic of beer—and Doyle mainly listened, since she didn't tend to keep up on such things.

Riordan complained, "The Rovers need some new blood, but the owner won't open his purse."

"The Kingsmen managed to steal Kariuki from Barcelona; he should rattle a few middies."

"Aye—the lad has promise," Riordan agreed.

"There'll never be another Rizzo, though," Grady declared with a full measure of regret. To Doyle, he asked, "Did they ever solve Rizzo's murder?" He then glanced over at Riordan to add, "He was killed in an RC Church, you know," just to get a bit of his own back.

"I don't think they have any leads," Doyle equivocated, and was yet again reminded of Sir Vikili's debt to Acton, which—mayhap—he'd paid off in this latest misadventure. Strange, how everything always seemed to circle back—even Maguire-the-ghost was a circle-back; there were some definite parallels betwixt the ghostly newsman and the Song plot, with the moral of the story being that it never paid to cross Acton.

Indeed, the whole situation was a reminder that the justice-system took a back seat to her husband's wishes, being as there was always the chance that the system might not punish those who'd caused harm to his wife severely enough. The beatitude may be 'blessed are the merciful' but it went without saying that there wasn't a whole lot of mercy, rattling about in Acton's soul.

Although mayhap she was being too hasty; after all, she'd jumped to the wrong conclusion about Acton's plans for Riordan—shame on her, for not being a bit more cautious, considering what was at stake—and now she'd have some explaining to do to her husband. No matter; she'd think of something so as to keep Riordan's secret—it was the least she could do.

CHAPTER 39

He almost couldn't believe his eyes. She was here. He issued some quick instructions to the asset on-site.

The train bound for northern parts was due in a few minutes, and Doyle stood with Riordan and Grady on the open platform as they waited for it. The air was chilly after the rain, and Doyle didn't have an overcoat—since the trip was spur-of the moment—and so Grady had given her his, with the result that the gamekeeper was trying not to shiver in his shirtsleeves.

"D'you have everythin' you need?" Doyle asked Riordan, wondering if she should stay to wave him off—she probably should, and it wouldn't be longer than a few more awkward minutes, after all.

"I do—the police booked me through to Dublin."

"Well, it's the least they can do, after havin' disrupted your life for this long. They'll be happy to see you again at the library."

Riordan smiled slightly. "That they will."

Faith, where is that train? thought Doyle; I'm running out of things to say for probably the first time in history.

As could be expected in a smaller town's station, the platform only boasted a scattering of people, and Doyle—after viewing the area with a police officer's eye—noted a man, sitting on one of the benches with his overcoat collar turned-up so that it half-obscured his face. He didn't have a suitcase or a valise—even though he appeared to be a businessman—and although he seemed to be sitting patiently, he was actually emanating anxiety.

"Watch out for him," Doyle advised Riordan in a low tone. "He's an odd one."

"Yes," he agreed. "Very worried about something."

I don't like this, Doyle decided, her instinct on high alert; there's something strange about this fellow. "Who's he?" she asked Grady, with a sidelong glance toward the seated figure. "D'you know?"

The gamekeeper gave the fellow a covert glance from beneath his brows. "No. Not a local, I think."

Strange—that someone who was not a local would be leaving this particular station in the late afternoon without any hand-luggage. Doyle was trying to decide whether she should just leave it be or walk over and sound him out when the decision was taken out of her hands, and the man rose to approach them.

"Stand ready," she advised Grady quietly. "This may be trouble."

"Yes, ma'am," Grady replied with a touch of surprise, and stepped closer to her.

But it appeared such precautions weren't necessary, because

the man only stopped before them and asked, "Pardon me; has the train to Liverpool come yet?"

"No, sir," said Grady. "Not as yet."

"Good," the man said with a smile. "You've a Code Five, here."

Doyle blinked, because the reference was to the police code for an undercover operation, and hard on this realization she could see that he wore an earpiece.

In the background, she could hear the train approaching and so she quickly took Riordan's arm. "Let's step back, a bit—I think I dropped my gloves."

Grady said in surprise, "I don't think you brought gloves, ma'am."

"Let's step back, though—"

She turned and pulled Riordan along with her, just as one of the porters suddenly darted from the station-house and charged toward them at full speed, seizing Riordan in his arms and trying to wrestle him back toward the tracks.

"Drop," Doyle shouted, still gripping Riordan's arm with both of her hands, and they all fell into a heap on the platform as the porter frantically tried to untangle himself. Grady yanked hard to pull the man from Doyle and—once free—he turned to race toward the oncoming train.

Two men had emerged from the station-house to give chase, but the porter managed to leap across the train tracks, barely clearing them before the oncoming train obscured all view of him.

"Go, go, go," the man dressed as a businessman urged into his communication device, and the two men scrambled down from the platform, having to wait for the train to come to a stop before giving chase.

"Stay down," Doyle instructed Riordan as she crouched

beside them. "It's a police operation." She looked up and then blinked hard, because—unless she was having another one of those reticulating-delirium-things—the overcoated figure of her wedded husband was approaching quickly down the platform.

Doyle scrambled to her feet. "Sir," she said, after deciding she should probably put on her detective-hat.

"You are unhurt?"

"Yes, sir." And then, unable to contain herself, she glanced over toward the train tracks. "Who was the perp?"

"Kirken," he replied. "We'd a trap-and-seizure in play."

The light dawned; that was why Riordan had been publicly booked on this train, to embark from this obscure little town; he'd been the bait to lure-in Kirken, and it all made perfect sense. Doyle closed her eyes briefly. "Faith, Michael—I'm that sorry I've mucked it up."

"No matter," he said. "I imagine he will be secured very shortly." To Riordan, he asked, "You are all right?"

"I am."

"You will be taken by private car to the ferry, if that is agreeable." Acton raised his gaze, and the faux-businessman willingly stepped forward. "I will see to it, sir."

Riordan blew out a breath. "Well, that was all very unexpected. Thank you, Lady Acton."

"Just returnin' the favor," she joked. "Now, back to Dublin with you."

"It has been a pleasure," he said in Gaelic, and it was true.

"It's definitely been something," she returned in the same language, and he smiled a bit ruefully.

Riordan was then escorted toward a waiting car, and Doyle stayed beside Acton, as he waited for word on the escaped suspect.

"There are men on the perimeter?" she ventured. This would

be the usual protocol, just in case things went sideways—with the current situation serving as an excellent example.

"Williams is here, with a team," he replied. "Kirken won't get far."

No, she thought, silently processing this disclosure. In fact, she'd be very much surprised if the aforesaid suspect survived this little take-down—after all, if Kirken lived, the artwork trial would be back on and the fair Doyle would have to take the stand. She'd been in enough of these situations with the man standing beside her to know he'd have spun an inescapable web, with every possible contingency accounted-for.

Save, of course, that he didn't think to account for his wayward wife's getting herself involved. With a sting of shame, she admitted that she should have realized there was a trap-and-seizure in play—which only went to show that her detective-brain was a bit rusty. After all, there'd been public rumors that Riordan was hiding-out at Trestles—not what you'd expect, with a protected witness—and then he was booked to travel on a public train—again, not something that would happen if you were following the protocols for a protected witness.

Meanwhile, it was public knowledge that Acton had been suspended from duty—no doubt that was all trumped-up, too, to try to get Kirken to take this prime opportunity to strike at Riordan, the only man left who could implicate him in the artwork-rig. And it had worked a charm; Kirken was desperate, and must have seen this opportunity as a godsend—he'd know exactly where Riordan would be, and at exactly what time.

And as for the CID, it was miles easier to bring charges for attempted murder—with so many witnesses to see—than it was to go after a judicial officer for questionable judicial conduct. Of course, the CID wouldn't be aware that Kirken wasn't slated to survive; they'd only see the trap-and-seizure for what it appeared to be, a good plan to catch an elusive criminal. They wouldn't know that the trap-and-seizure was actually a trap-and-execute, in true Acton-fashion. What had Maguire said? "All tracks neatly covered; all problems neatly eliminated." And the ghost was right; he wrote an exposé on the subject, after all.

One thing didn't make sense though, and she ventured, "I wish you'd have told me, Michael—I would have steered well-clear."

In an apologetic tone, her husband replied, "It had to be kept very quiet, because Kirken has contacts within law enforcement." He paused. "And I will admit it did not occur to me that you would show up on-scene."

She winced. "Clompin' about, like a cow in a cornfield. I'm truly sorry, Michael."

"No matter," he soothed, and smiled into her eyes. But even as she smiled back, she could sense that he was sorely disappointed.

CHAPTER 40

The two ghosts stood together in the stacks at Trinity College Library, watching Seamus Riordan as he methodically cross-checked his filings.

The first ghost—who wore academic robes from a bygone period—said to Maguire, "Well done, and greatly appreciated, sir. It wouldn't have been fair, after he'd gathered-up his courage to go forth and right the wrongs."

Maguire nodded, as his gaze rested upon Riordan. "No—it wouldn't have been fair. And it's just as well that she's none the wiser about what her husband had planned."

"Little chance of that," the other ghost observed with a trace of derision. "She's got the sense of a gnat."

But Maguire shook his head a bit gravely. "She knows her husband, though—knows him well. And it's something he does on the regular—sets it up so that they'd both be killed, with none to see that it was all his doing."

Made a bit anxious by the words, the other ghost ventured, "I can't think he'd try again, though; he'd run the risk that she will realize."

Maguire let out a breath. "He plays the long game. I'm afraid we can only wait and hope."

With a nod, the other ghost returned his gaze to the young librarian. "I wish the lad had never met the sister. I worry that there's trouble, ahead."

"There's not much we can do about that. Hopefully, time and distance will do its work."

"Women," the first ghost observed in disapproval.

"Not all women," Maguire pointed out. "I wouldn't have been able to get him back here without her help."

"I suppose," the other reluctantly conceded. "But she's so—so common. Common, and not very clever—I've no idea what he sees in her."

But Maguire only smiled. "I do," he said.

CHAPTER 41

In a strange way, he was relieved. Relieved and frustrated. What to do?

They'd come home, after Acton and his team had released the site and had held a debriefing with the local team. From what Doyle had gleaned, Kirken had taken his own life once he was cornered—which was something of interest, in that you'd think if the man had been carrying a gun he'd of used it on Riordan.

In any event, there was no chance whatsoever that Acton would have allowed Kirken to survive, and so she should probably be grateful that they'd brushed though it as well as they had. At least now she'd not have to testify—not to mention that Seamus Riordan was going back to where he belonged, safe and sound; there was nothing worse, when good people came forward to hold the villains accountable but then were made to suffer for it.

They'd arrived back at the flat after the boys were already

abed, and Doyle was unsurprised when Acton said he'd need to retreat to his office to make a report. He'd been quiet on the ride home, and she was well-familiar with the signs that indicated he was wrestling with his demons, and trying to hide it from her.

In truth, it was his usual pattern; he'd capably managed the dismantling of a potential disaster and—now that there was no longer a crisis to navigate—he'd withdraw with a bottle of scotch to drink steadily—sometimes not coming to bed a'tall.

Acton was one who preferred to face his demons alone, but he'd a mad Irish bride who knew how to draw him out of the dismals, and good luck to the man if he was hoping she'd act sensibly, for once.

Therefore, after waiting a goodly space of time—her ministrations were always more effective after he was a bit bosky—she slipped through his office door, and closed it behind her. "Need some company?"

He was seated with his desk chair turned around so that he could gaze out into the night sky as he cradled a glass in his hand. He didn't stand or turn to face her—which was a tell-tale sign that he was well into the bottle; Acton always had impeccable manners.

"No," he said.

She said softly, "Now, there's brusque, if I ever heard it."

He leaned forward, and rubbed his face with his hands. Poor man, she thought; he's of two minds—he wishes I'd leave and he hopes I'll stay.

"Can we talk a bit?" she ventured. "It won't be a discussion, I promise."

"I am not good company, Kathleen."

"As though that's ever stopped me, husband."

He continued silent, leaning forward with his head bowed and his hands clasped between his knees.

"I'll let you feel the bump on my head, if you'd like."

He glanced around at her, amused despite himself. "Why did you come to Trestles, Kathleen?"

Readily, she answered, "I found out Riordan had been hidden-away there, and I decided that I should go thank him in person for savin' my life—it's the same as I felt about thankin' the nurses."

She paused, and then added, "I'm that sorry I mucked-up your take-down, Michael, after all your careful plannin'. But I suppose it can be chalked-up as a success in the end; saved the public the cost of Kirken's trial, and saved me and Sir Vikili from brusquin' at each other in a court of law."

"Yes," he agreed, and turned to face the window again.

She was a bit surprised to note that this wasn't necessarily true—apparently, he didn't feel the takedown was a success. But that was no doubt because he didn't like it when things went sideways and got messy, which only reminded her that she'd some scolding to do, and best get on with it.

She came around to kneel before him, and lift his hands so as to take them in hers. Looking up into his face, she said, "I'm goin' to browbeat you a bit, Michael—but not too much; you've had a 'trying time'—whatever that means."

He made a sound of impatience. "You are the one who almost died, Kathleen."

"Not that I'm aware, Michael—'tis you that bore the brunt of it." She paused. "And then hard on that disaster, Song tried to blackmail you."

He stilled.

"Faith, what are the odds that I'd have an Irish nurse, who must have had someone similar in the family tree? I'm that sorry to bring even more trouble atop the first, Michael."

"Don't," he protested, just as she knew he would. "You bear no blame."

"Aye, but you do bear a burden, my friend. I know that the disasters were pilin' up, but you can't go about killin' people. Life's a complicated kettle-o'-snakes, and nothing's ever as simple as it looks to be; you decide to pull one straw from the pile but then the whole thing might collapse in a heap. You can't always account for the fall-out, just as you can't out-dance the devil—no matter how good your intentions."

He tilted his head slightly. "I might beg to disagree."

This, of course, had been shown to be true—or at least, often enough in her unexpected marriage—and so she decided to say a bit more firmly, "The point is this, Michael; it's not the right way to go about things. You need only look to scripture; there's story after story about people who got their comeuppance for tryin' to take things into their own hands." She paused. "Although to be fair, I suppose there's more than a few preemption-murders that worked-out, too. Judith, for one—cut off that fellow's head."

He smiled slightly. "Indeed."

Much encouraged by this response, she continued, "But the point remains, Michael, that you shouldn't go about killin' people because you're afraid they'll escape their just desserts— or they'll expose somethin' that you don't want exposed. Instead, you're supposed to err on the side of mercy and trust God to get it right—just like David did with King Saul. I know it's rough—especially if it looks as though you're headin' for a nasty disaster. But life's more complicated than we can ever imagine, and you're supposed to trust that God understands it all, and knows what He's doin'."

"I am afraid I cannot aspire to such," he admitted.

Doyle decided it was not worth trying to translate this dose of aristo-speak, and instead deemed that she'd said enough—it was not as though he hadn't heard it all before, and it did seem as though the black mood wasn't hovering quite so close.

In an encouraging tone—much the same as Maguire had used with her—she offered, "Well, despite the occasional misstep you've come a long way, Michael; I'm that proud of you. We just need to smooth out the rough edges at bit; you're the flawed champion in this story, and we can't expect miracles."

At that, he lifted his gaze to meet hers. "On the contrary, it did seem a miracle."

He seemed to be referring to her rescue, and she decided she'd best avoid the subject lest he start to wonder why Seamus Riordan's instinct had been so spot-on. And so instead, she said, "Aye—things were grim, until your staunch supporters made a stand and fought like the dickens. Lucky for you, that you've some trusty sidekicks."

"More like it is you, who have trusty sidekicks."

She smiled. "Well, I'm *your* trusty sidekick, and so it all amounts to the same thing. And speakin' of which, remember when you used to hound me for sex?"

His gaze held hers for a silent moment. "I wouldn't necessarily say I *hounded* you."

"Well, I would. Not that it's anythin' but a distant memory."

He confessed, "I am not certain I am capable, at the moment."

"Let's test it out. I'll lock the door and you start thinkin' lustful thoughts."

He took the hands that held his, kissed them, and then pressed them against either side of his face. "I don't deserve you."

"Well, you've got me, whether it's deservin' or not. Now

clear your desk, husband, and let's get to it. Try not to wake the boyos, please."

"I'm not the noisy one," he reminded her, as he rose rather unsteadily to his feet.

"Well, we'll just have to see about that," she replied, and moved to lock the door.

Made in the USA
Middletown, DE
02 May 2025